Lavender and Haddock

Part One of the
'Trouble with Wyrms'
Trilogy

Mike Williams

Text and Cover Illustrations Copyright © 2015 Mike Williams

All rights reserved.

ISBN-10: 151684498X
ISBN-13: 978-1516844982

DEDICATION

To 'grown-up' people everywhere who have never grown up.

CONTENTS

	Acknowledgments	i
	Introduction	1
1	Sodden-On-The-Bog	5
2	An Abundance of Tweed	18
3	Something Nasty in the Bathroom	36
4	The Vicar's Great Plan	47
5	A Rat in a Trap	58
6	Enter the Dragon	70
7	The Grouse Shoot	85
	Character List	97
	About the Author	99

ACKNOWLEDGMENTS

A very special thanks to my long-suffering friends who instead of drinking their pints in one gulp and fleeing from the pub, were always there to listen to my stories - or perhaps they were sloshed.

INTRODUCTION

'*The Trouble with Wyrms*' was hardly the most riveting title for an evening's entertainment at the church hall, but it was better than most. There had been '*Lavender and Haddock*', a collection of beauty tips for the over-seventies that had sent the over sixties bachelors fleeing to the pub. '*Memoires of a Fox Hunting Lady*' had to be cancelled because she'd forgotten, whilst the only charitable thing to say about '*Cocksfoot and Timothy*' was that it was short, full of botanical insight and had attracted the wrong sort of audience altogether.

But the ladies of the town were a forgiving bunch. What else was there to do of an evening with the old man in the pub and the supper pots washed? Why, you might as well wrap up warm, reach for the umbrella and brave the damp, dirty air for the excitement of the hall and the promise of tea and cakes. Besides, tonight there was a hint of mystery, an outside speaker, a certain *Professor Arbutus Broadbent, MSc, Ph.D. and Friend of the Fyshes*, whatever that meant. Whatever indeed, for some of the audience the explanation was obvious. But these were strangers to the town and seated at the front; forty freshly-scrubbed women dressed in tweeds and sensible shoes and looking exactly the same, if not decidedly out of place.

There was a hush in the hall as a rather white-faced, perspiring gentleman dressed in linen and leather patches stood up to the podium. The poor man fumbled with his papers and taking a fountain pen from his top pocket, pretended to make various important changes to various important points in his talk, while all the time ticking off names. They were all here he noted, thank the heavens, but others too, an extra audience he hadn't counted on. If anything he had tried his damnedest to put them off. *The Trouble with Wyrms*, he thought as he had penned the notice for the Derbyshire Clarion, Manchester Evening News and other worthy papers. What a perfect title, what a guaranteed, sleep-inducing, stay-away-in-droves, have-better-things-to-do-than-listen-to-this-sort-of-rubbish, banner of a headline. Except it had proven the opposite and here was the problem, and it made him uneasy. He poured himself a glass of water from a chipped enamel jug but thought better of taking a sip. The words *'Co-op Dairies-TB or not TB, We Know the Answer,'* were printed on the side and there was a scum of insect remains floating on the surface, with whatever had eaten the most of them swimming on the bottom.

'He's a fussy one,' whispered a local woman to her neighbour at the back of the hall. 'I only changed the water last month, fresh it was too, straight from the font.'

'Stands to reason,' whispered her neighbour. 'Our Moira had her youngest christened last week and she piddled a river!' The two ladies burst into laughter.

The professor, for he was the unfortunate gentleman, did his best to ignore the giggles. He adjusted his shirt cuffs as though it was a stage direction in bold type. A dramatic gesture with arms held aloft, the glint of silver cufflinks, the wave of a spotted silk handkerchief and he was about to begin. 'My dear friends,' he cried with much affection and wiping of the eyes. 'Welcome to England!'

There were wild cheers of approval, the sound of forty pairs of feet stamping in delight. 'Bravo, Professor! Bravo!' shouted the formidable women, with one or two throwing their hats into the air. 'Three cheers for Arbutus Broadbent! Hip, hip, hooray!' It was all rather confusing.

'They're a lively lot at the front,' whispered one late arrival, 'and what's all this stuff about England?'

The lady who had changed the water in the jug hadn't a clue. 'Don't ask me,' she said. 'I thought it was going to be your Elsie talking about rhubarb jam, not this old chap.'

'Didn't you read the poster? It's some professor from across the moors. He's here to tell us about worms.'

'Worms? Who wants to hear about worms?' dismissed the woman craning her neck like a submarine's periscope and scanning the room. 'And that lively lot at the front', she said in a voice too loud for polite enquiry.

'Not from around here are they?'

They were certainly not. The ladies in tweed were strangers to the village, each having arrived from somewhere a little to the left and slightly to the south of the buckle on Orion's belt. They turned as one and stared at the people at the back, making them feel as though they were naughty little children at least. There was an air of authority in the strangers' dress and in the peculiar way they seemed to look all the same. If the local women only knew what they were up against they would have fled the hall, dragged their husbands out of the pub and caught the next available boat train to France. Take the unfortunate shepherd now half man, half scarecrow left dangling

LAVENDER AND HADDOCK

on the moor, his arms stretched out and with crows pecking at his ears. All he was doing was minding his own business, leaning on his crook and smoking his pipe, when a hole had ripped open in the sky and a column of substantial women had marched forth. 'Blimey,' he had said with a dirty leer on his face. 'There's more shags 'ere than the cliffs of Dover.' It was a pity he'd been overheard, and by a witch with a phrasebook.

'Sisters, my dear Sisters' continued the professor feeling more confident by the minute. 'What a glorious day it is to see you all here safe! Welcome to your new home!'

'What did he say?' asked the ever inquisitive woman at the back, nudging her neighbour yet again. 'He's getting a bit fresh with them at the front isn't he?'

'He's offered them his home. He thinks he's a bleedin' maharajah!' And the two ladies laughed even more.

The professor seemed agitated. He looked at the many faces in the church hall and frowned. 'There are strangers here; we must be careful,' he said lowering his voice and leaning further over the podium until it seemed he would tumble forward into the front row. 'Sisters we must be cautious. There are spies everywhere, and if the Big Secret is to remain a big secret then...'

'Sssshhhh!' hissed forty pairs of lips with forty fingers placed in front, and the professor stepped back in surprise. 'Oh!' he said, realising his mistake. 'Of course, how stupid of me. I forgot. One must never mention the...'

'Sssshhhh!'

'Absolutely, I shall...'

'Ssssshhhh!'

'Enough!' implored the professor. 'Please, enough with the shushing.' He was wiping his face with his handkerchief. 'My dear Sisters, you have made your point, there's no need for this...this moisture! May I suggest one small thing, in the interest of getting the meeting off to a start?' He made a circular motion with his finger as though he was stirring a large cup of tea. 'A little of the old magic don't you think?'

The ladies tapped their noses and winked at the professor. Forty cheroots appeared from forty purses and with a click of forty pairs of fingers, sprung to light.

'You'd think they'd offer them around', sighed the woman at the back. 'I could kill for a Woodbine.' But before she could continue with her carping and complaining, she found herself waking up in an empty church hall with a monstrous headache and the faintest wisp of purple smoke curling upwards to the ceiling.

And that is how this tale began...or was it? What a pity no one had asked the caveman. 'Ugg!' he had shouted as he danced frantically around the cavewoman, and her with a baby on each breast and his mother chewing leather by the fire. 'Ouch!' he had cried as the rock she threw hit him squarely on the head. The poor man, he was waving his arms and pointing to the valley below, but his vocabulary was all winter solstice, and if the poor woman had had enough of one thing, it was winter solstice. She'd two twins and another on the way from all that nonsense.

'Ugg!' he said and dodged a second rock. It was a question of vocabulary. What he was trying to say was 'Grab the kids and let's get out of here!' Unfortunately, so many 'Uggs' and a few cartwheels around the fire could also mean 'Brace yourself hot lips, I feel a Neanderthal coming on,' and trust a woman to think the worst. Only when he had sulked off to the back of the cave and had daubed paint on the walls were the archaeologists to catch on. So much for the giant meteor, the lizards were back. There was a wormhole in space leaking dragons into his valley.

Chapter One

SODDEN-ON-THE-BOG

If you drive north through Derbyshire with your foot pressed firmly down on the pedal, the scenery will suddenly change. Large gaps will start to appear in the tidy gritstone walls, the air will get noticeably thin and if you wait long enough, the occasional hang glider will fall from the sky only to be pounced upon by half-starved sheep or locals desperate for conversation. You will have reached Grimspittle Moor – a blank on the map marked *'Here be Germs'*. The Romans had lasted there for three weeks, the Danes for less, and if historians are to be believed even Bonny Prince Charlie turned back in disgust after drinking a pint of green ale in 'The Lamb and Liver Fluke.' For it was neither the mud nor poor tactics that put paid to him at Culloden, merely a lack of dock leaves and privacy.

A few miles further north and you will have arrived at the infamous Grimspittle reservoir; a large expanse of thick brown water on which the occasional coot or mallard may squawk in surprise then disappear forever beneath the surface. Anglers have been known to drop their sandwiches and run away in fear from their catch while only the bravest of divers dare to dip their fins and risk being mistaken for a large black pudding. These are haunted waters where less than a hundred years ago stood a proud but isolated village called Sodden-on-the-Bog. During long hot summers when the water level falls, it is possible to see the cracked and bent spire of the village church. In drier years where only a greasy pool remains in the centre, the ruins of a large manor house can be seen in the sun-baked mud. There are even reports of strange tracks in the silt, as though a large creature with tentacles had dragged itself out of the building to the shallow waters nearby. It is rumoured even that the museum in Buxton holds a collection of plaster casts of the same, but try asking one of the attendants. They will shrug their shoulders and usher you towards a boring vase in the corner that Romans used to spit in. It is as though Miss Arabella Pike had not existed at all.

Miss Arabella Pike was a mystery. No one in Sodden could remember how long she had lived in the manor house nor what she had done in the past to have amassed what was commonly talked about in the tap room of 'The Lamb and Liver Fluke' as a 'fair bit of brass and no mistake'. To be fair to the villagers they left her well alone. She was courteous, rich and prompt in payment, not qualities shared by many. Who wouldn't forgive her the occasional eccentricity, her monocle or her cigars? There was also the question of her pet – a subject of much speculation ever since Bad Phlegm the Burglar had dropped his trousers in court and pointing to the teeth marks on his leg, had demanded compensation or at least some ointment. Although no one had set eyes on the animal, it was the considered opinion of many, including the postman, that she had rescued it from a zoo – most probably after the creature had eaten its way through half the Serengeti with a couple of keepers thrown in for pudding. One can imagine therefore the interest in the village when it was discovered Miss Pike had a sister, a twin sister at that, who not only dressed the same in tweeds and sensible shoes, but lived closeby in the mill town of Frogwallop.

'I could have sworn it were Miss Pike if I'd not seen 'em together,' the landlord of 'The Lamb and Liver Fluke', George Stubbins, recounted to his regular customers. 'As alike as two peas in a pod they were, with Miss Pike ordering t'other one about with the shopping. And that's another thing,' he continued to his eager audience. 'You should've seen what they carried out from the butchers, a great big side of beef. All that for the two of them? I don't think so. I bet it were for the pet.'

At this information, a few of the men at the bar cast worried glances at each other. The postman began to shake so much that his beer splashed in all directions, and a swarthy looking stranger in a striped jersey threw his bag out the window and gave himself up to the police.

'I'd say we're in for some right funny goings on, you mark my words'. But hardly had the landlord begun to speak than the door to the pub swung open and with a flurry of fallen leaves Miss Arabella Pike walked in. She nodded to each of the customers in turn, shook her umbrella dry and ordered a pint of ale.

It would be unfair to call 'The Lamb and Liver Fluke' old fashioned, this being 1912 after all. Yet the sight of Miss Pike pulling up a stool and gulping down the best half of her drink without so much as a hairbrush, a hand mirror or a breath of fresh air, made a few of the regulars uneasy. It wasn't that she was sitting in the wrong bar, although the lounge was far more suitable and even had the occasional bottle of cherry brandy on the shelf. What caused the many 'um's', diddledy-dees' and furtive explorations of the handkerchief was the sheer size and presence of the lady. Despite her middle years she still possessed what may be described as an agricultural beauty – a trait too often overlooked by handsome city folk but highly prized here in the village. The size of her hands alone was a wonder to many, 'two cows a minute' being a whispered phrase. For if men's thoughts could be read that night it would be no surprise to find visions of autumn marriage, bumper milk yields and stooks of oats being tossed far and high over ribbon-decked carts.

Miss Pike was oblivious to her charms. She had spent a hectic day packing clothes, books and other essentials into numerous trunks before sending them on to the village station, all because of a troubling and frightened telephone call she had received the night before. She was now trying to collect her thoughts over a quiet pint of ale before her train was due and didn't care to be disturbed by any idle chitter-chatter. But if George Stubbins had one failing in life then it was gossip. His small world was a circular jigsaw of the village with the pieces so similarly shaped that they could be arranged in any fashion. That often the final picture made no sense was not for want of George's shuffling and thumping the pieces to fit. With this rare visit of the mysterious Miss Pike to his bar, who could blame him for attempting the most difficult section first, that part of the puzzle which was sea, sky or in this case tweed. He stood staring and smiling at the lady, his fingers nervously stroking his moustache as he thought of an opening gambit.

'It'll be nice for you to have your sister living near,' he began, affecting an air of innocence. But Arabella merely looked at him in puzzlement and reaching in her handbag pulled out a long thin cigar and a box of matches. She proceeded to light the cigar and blow small red smoke rings to the ceiling.

'Cuban is it?' inquired George amazed at the colour of the smoke and the faint smell of kippers sizzling in a pan.

'Vermillion,' corrected Arabella with what she could manage of a smile.

'Oh I see, Russian,' continued George in total ignorance, 'that would explain the colour wouldn't it. As for me I prefer a pipe, that's if the missus allows.'

Arabella nodded in sympathy and blew a bright purple square skidding along the bar.

'That's some rum tobacco that is.' But as much as this new mystery intrigued George, the question of the twin sister in Frogwallop had to be answered. 'So how's your sister settling in then? It's a fair big place she's got in town. Used to belong to an admiral, or was it an army gentleman? Someone in a uniform anyway.'

'Sister, Mr Stubbins? What are you talking about?'

'Not that I'm nosey like, but the missus said how she'd seen you and your sister moving furniture into that big house off the high street. So I said to her, it would be nice for Miss Pike to have a bit of company, what with you living up at the manor house on your own.'

'I think you must be referring to my friend, Mr Stubbins.'

'Well, there's a funny coincidence…'

'What is?'

'That you two are so alike.'

'Really? I don't think so; we're entirely different.'

Unfortunately, George was distracted from his conversation by the postman ordering another drink. He frowned as he pulled the pint, not liking his quest for information interrupted, but was surprised to find on being given the money a small piece of crumpled paper on which was written in spidery scrawl the words…

'*Ask her about the meat.*'

One can only admire the skill and tact of George's next ploy, particularly so since brilliant green smoke was being blown into perfectly formed triangles above his head.

'Well, you two won't be starving this winter, what with all that beef. The missus said she could feed a circus for a year on what you were carrying out of the butchers. I bet your dog'll be appreciating the bones.'

'Dog, Mr Stubbins? What dog? I can't abide the lop-tongued, silly creatures.'

Before George could ask about the possibility of cats, large jungle ones at that with bits of corduroy trousers stuck between their teeth, the station boy put his head around the door and called for Miss Pike. She quickly finished the remainder of her drink and after bidding everyone goodnight left to catch her train.

'And there you are,' said George in answer to the knowing looks from his regulars. 'Still none the wiser are we.' He wiped the surface of the counter with his apron before noticing the still lit cigar smouldering and spitting in the ashtray. After checking that no one was looking he placed it between his lips. The postman was aware of someone tapping him on the shoulder. He looked up to see a smiling George with two pint glasses stuck under his jumper.

'Hello, big boy,' George quipped sucking on the cigar, but instead of blowing out a trail of geometric shapes, he gulped, coughed and staring with intense concentration at a small speck of dirt on the opposite wall, fell like an upturned plank to the floor.

Arabella had the carriage to herself and sufficient time before she reached Frogwallop to think over her predicament. The trouble had begun with a telephone call from her friend the night before, far too soon after falling asleep. Not being used to 3 o'clock in the morning, Arabella had found herself bumping into furniture in search of her monocle and the brass telephone in the hall. After stubbing her toe on the doorframe and mistakenly putting a bracelet in her mouth and a top set of dentures around her wrist, she was now composing a choice phrase or two to greet her inconsiderate caller. Before she could launch into a scathing response, Arabella was cut short by a heartfelt cry from her friend in Frogwallop, Rowena Carp.

'Thank heavens you've answered. Something terrible has happened. I've just seen a beard and whiskers in the mirror!'

Arabella sat down in a chair and tried to clear her mind. 'Which mirror would that be Rowena dear?'

'The silver hand mirror, what else would I be talking about!'

'Did you try that ointment I bought for you? The Chemist assured me it was just the ticket.'

'Not my face, someone else's and, what's more, the glass has gone cloudy. I can't see a thing through it!'

'Are you sure dear?' Arabella replied. 'Have you tried shaking it?'

'Only for the past ten minutes.'

'What about giving it a little bash, it could be the reception.' The sound of breaking glass and tears could be heard on the other end of the line.

'Please don't tell me you've broken it. You know how the Professor values them so.'

'No, I haven't,' snapped Rowena before sobbing uncontrollably. 'But Demetrios is chewing the goldfish. Oh, Arabella, this is impossible!'

'Look, dear, the first thing you must do is calm down. I can't understand you at all in this state.'

'Yes,' choked Rowena through her tears, 'I suppose you're right.'

'Good, that's better. Now, tell me again, but slowly this time – what exactly happened when you took the mirror out of its bag?'

'Well, I know I shouldn't have looked in the mirror, but I do miss home and I so wanted to see the mountains again. But this time all I could make out were bricks and drain pipes and dirty rats everywhere. Then a face appeared, snarling at me with horrid teeth. I was so scared that I dropped the mirror on the floor. I couldn't bring myself to pick it up again until now…'

'Rowena, this is important,' interrupted Arabella. 'How long was the mirror left out of its bag?'

'I did have a glass of whisky to calm my nerves…'

'Rowena?'

'It couldn't have been more than a few hours at the most. I'll put it back now if you like.'

Arabella was furious. She tried to count to ten but failed after three.

'Oh you silly woman, it's far too late. Do you have any idea of the damage you've done? Whoever was looking at you has had plenty of time to pinpoint our position. We are only supposed to use the mirrors when our task here is complete. You were told of this before. The boy is hardly thirteen. It's too soon Rowena, too soon!'

'Excuse me, Madam.' Arabella was woken up from her thoughts by the ticket collector gently shaking her arm. 'Frogwallop, Madam. You asked me to tell you when we were approaching the station.' Arabella thanked the collector and waited for the train to stop. She could make out the figure of her friend in the darkness waving at her from the platform.

'Guard!' she called as she stepped out of the carriage. 'Would you be so kind as to put my luggage on the Grubdale train for tomorrow morning? My name is Arabella Pike and the Station Master has been informed. If there are any problems I can be contacted at the *Butchers Apron*, I shall be staying there overnight,' and with these instructions she marched purposely past Rowena but not without a hissed remark. 'You're too conspicuous! Burn everything and meet me on the morning train and for heaven's sake get rid of that silly disguise. There's only one Queen Victoria and she's been dead for years.'

George Stubbins awoke the next morning with a head like a hamster spinning an empty dustbin along the cobbles, all the more painful for his wife screaming at him from downstairs to get up. Perhaps screaming was an understatement; Mrs Stubbins was in hysterics. She was balancing on a stool and swiping at something large and hairy that was snapping at her ankles. You could describe the thing as a rat, but of such a size that Dropkick the pub cat and champion mouser was clinging on to Mrs Stubbins' hair by its claws. As witness to the ferocity of the beast, which was now chewing the legs of the stool and spitting out splinters the size of tooth picks, Scutt the pub terrier and champion ratter had disgraced himself on the cold stone floor. He was now whining and howling in fear from on top of the cat. Nor was George spared from such bravery, entering as he did three times to the kitchen – once to see the rat, twice to look at it again, and the third time to poke at it from behind the door with two broom handles tied together.

'Don't prod it, hit the horrid thing!' his wife pleaded, but George could do neither. The rat had grasped the broom handle in its teeth and was now pulling him into the kitchen with each successive tug. Yet just as George was thinking of letting go and changing into something other than a cotton nightshirt tied up between his legs, the stool broke and put paid to the rat by the bulk of Mrs Stubbins landing on top. It was a fleeting impact. As soon as her bottom touched the floor and her newly acquired hairstyle in the shape of the cat and dog had rushed upstairs, Mrs Stubbins was up like a shot and half way down the high street before she realised what she was running through. In the brief moment it took George to stand up and prod the flattened beast a final time, his wife was back in the house locking all the doors and windows and mewing like a frightened kitten.

'Send a letter to the council,' she managed to whisper to George. 'There's a bleeding plague of them!' For outside in the main street Sodden was awash with vermin of all shapes and sizes, sniffing and scuttling from one house to another.

'Here, let me have a look,' said George pushing past her and peering through the hall window. 'Well I'll be....it's the drains, that's what it is. I thought I could smell something nasty the other morning. They must've been breeding there for years.'

'George,' whimpered his wife clinging to him for safety. 'Look at those big buggers there.'

George turned his head to the direction she was pointing and gasped in disbelief. Amid the swarm of rats stood five or six that were three foot tall.

'Bloody hell old girl, go and get my gun from under the bed.'
It seemed that some on the street had the same idea. Out of a few bedroom windows poked a collection of shotguns, catapults and in the case of the vicarage a shower of religious books thrown with surprising accuracy. It was hardly a fair fight, and after a few minutes most of the rats had disappeared leaving behind a scene like a kitchen in a bad restaurant.

There was no sign of the larger rats. It seemed they had fled in the direction of the moor when the shooting had begun. So George took it upon himself to take control of the situation. After dressing in a thick pair of moleskin trousers tied up at the ankles with numerous pieces of string and collecting his less than enthusiastic dog from out of the airing cupboard, George marched into the middle of the street and organised a small posse of villagers around him. 'Us three will take the road past Miss Pike's house,' he said pointing to two young lads fresh out of bed. 'And you Vicar can lift the lid off that drain and crucify anything that jumps out. Tie those trouser legs tight boys; these aren't your average rat. They'll be up and through your undercarriage like a doctor's thermometer, if you'll pardon the expression Vicar.' So with new found courage courtesy of a glass of brandy handed out on a tin tray by his wife, George and the young lads marched up the road with shotgun and cudgels at the ready.

'Remember boys, if I miss with the first shot you won't be running away now, will you?'

As they approached the top of the street and passed the wall to Arabella's garden, they became aware of a tall, stout stranger watching them from the gate. He was dressed in a large, neatly tailored black coat that reached almost to his feet. His face was obscured by both the shadow of his bowler hat and prominent side whiskers, but it seemed to George that he was smiling. In his hand was a long black cane tipped with a silver claw, which he raised in greeting. Scutt the terrier ran up to the stranger and after sniffing at his shoes skulked back to the safety of his owner and growled half-heartedly.

'Morning,' greeted George as they passed the stranger. 'Take no notice of the dog; it's not right in the head that one.' The stranger nodded his head and watched them walk away up the street.

'Now there's a proper gentleman,' assured George to the two lads. 'You can tell from the cut of his coat. We should have more like him in the village. Expensive drinks he buys I bet, and lots of 'em.'

The two lads murmured in agreement, which said a lot about their tailors but considerably less about their eyesight. For if they had only stopped to shake hands with this stranger they would have noticed his one calloused claw and a sharpened silver hook where the other had been. They would have stared at his cruel eyes spaced too far apart. They would have galled at his teeth protruding like two yellowed chisels from under his top lip, and if they had shaken his 'hand' for too long the last sound they would have heard would be a 'thud' as something long and thick and not unlike a rat's tail would have hit the floor from behind. For this was Vermyn Stench, recently arrived on the planet, head of the secret police and second only to the great sorcerer Tarantulas Spleen in his hatred of all things 'tweed.'

When the trio had disappeared from view and Vermyn was convinced no one else was looking, he opened the gate to Arabella's house and strode along the cobbled path to the front door. He raised his head sniffing each of the wooden panels from top to bottom, before turning to face the garden and tapping his cane sharply once, on the path. To his side appeared four large rats, each over 3ft tall and armed with cruel twisted knives. He smiled a brief, fleeting grin then swung his cane around his head and smashed the silver claw against the door. With a loud 'crack' the lock and hinges shattered and the rats, screaming with excitement, ran scuttling into the house. They searched each room in turn, leaving behind a collection of smashed furniture and shredded linen, but found no trace of Arabella or any clue as to where she had fled. They were not entirely alone. Whatever had chewed on Bad Phlegm's leg and had enjoyed a diet of fresh raw beef was now waiting for them, silent and salivating in the underground river that ran through the cellar.

Krek, the largest and most observant of the four rats, was the first to notice the hidden door in the wall. He tugged at the tail of Vermyn's coat and pointed with his knife at the keyhole just visible in the wooden panelling. Vermyn approached the door and felt for its outline, then chattering with frustration knelt down on one knee and sniffed at the lock. He fell back in disgust, holding his claw in front of his nose and blinking as his eyes watered. There was an unforgettable smell of something large and reptilian on the other side. Clicking and chattering at the four rats, he made them chew and claw their way through the flimsy woodwork and walk on ahead down the cellar steps. They too could make out the smell and seemed reluctant to go on any further.

Krek turned to face his leader and made the sign of the snake with a frantic twitching of his claws. The other three hissed and squealed in fear, repeating over and over again to each other the sign of the snake and huddling closer to Krek for safety. Vermyn snarled, spat and waved his cane in front of their terrified faces, but the rats refused to move. The one creature they feared most was 'snake'. Too often had they seen their lesser countrymen stabbed, squeezed and swallowed like velvet-covered cherries picked from a bowl. Humans were different, humans were stupid. They could be made to scream and dance with a touch of a claw or the whip of a tail, but snakes? No, snakes were terrible in their hunger. One minute you'd be grooming your fur and thinking how attractive your sisters looked, the next you'd feel a sharp stabbing pain in the back of your neck, your conversation would disintegrate to dribble, and before long you'd be bumping your nose on a viper's epiglottis, if there was such a thing, no one having survived to tell the tale.

All of these excuses took time to explain, especially in sign language and particularly so when the symbol for 'sister' could look disturbingly like 'brother' in the heat of the moment. But the creature the rats feared most was standing in front, snarling and spitting in anger at being disobeyed. Vermyn Stench had not been appointed head of the secret police for drinking tea from a china cup with his little pinkie curled. He wiped the blood off his silver claw and kicked aside the now ripped and leaking body of Krek, gesturing in no uncertain terms for the other three to continue, with himself three steps behind of course.

As the morning train for Grubdale left the station platform, Arabella could make out the smoke and flame of a distant fire through the carriage window. It seemed as though Rowena had kept to her part of the plan, even though she had failed to appear on the station platform as arranged.

'My, my, will you look at that,' exclaimed a military looking gentleman seated opposite. 'Native uprising, what?' He chuckled and took a swig of whisky from a hip flask before offering it to Arabella. She declined, not out of politeness or the hour of the morning, but because she could make out every detail of a hurried breakfast in the whiskers on his chin. 'Suit yourself,' he continued replacing the flask back in his jacket pocket. Arabella smiled then closed her eyes and feigned sleep, but it was too late, she was a captive audience.

'I met a man once who'd escaped a fire. Legs burnt to a crisp and still smoking they were too. Africa, it was. Silly bugger, he'd been trying to impress a beauty in the long grass with a touch of the Baden Powells.'

Arabella opened her eyes.

'Got you!' he laughed, pointing his fingers at her like a pistol. 'You know the sort of thing, scout's stuff, a rubbing of the sticks and a blowing like crazy.' He chuckled at his description then clapped his hands together. 'Whoompf! Set the whole riverbank on fire he did - too much paraffin and too little sense. Three villages, two legs and one maiden's honour – not bad for a mornings work, what!' He continued to laugh at his story then wiping his eyes with a handkerchief, returned his attention to the carriage window.

'Looks like a big fire. You can still see it from here.'

They continued awhile in silence, the only noise being the regular thump of the wheels on the track until the gentleman thought of another amusing tale.

'Never trust an elephant. Shot one once, bloody missed.'

Arabella smoothed down her coat and smiled out of politeness.

'Saw Jumbo two years later in a circus, all dressed up to the nines in silks and glitter, and balancing on a ball. Damn fine act until he cast an eye in my direction.' He started to laugh and slapped his knees in delight. 'Big bugger recognised me, didn't he!'

Arabella had to admit the story had merit.

'Mind you, it's one thing being charged by an elephant in the bush, but in a big top in Clapham? Well, there's a first for you - Jumbo chasing after me on a ball, those big elephant feet going like the clappers!' The gentleman drummed his fingers on his lap in imitation. 'Hannibal crossing the Alps, what!'

Seeing that he was laughing on his own, he tried to calm down and continue the conversation in a more serious vein. 'Funny thing, I was the star of the show that night.' For some reason or other this part of the story upset him. He opened his newspaper and attempted to read a particularly boring paragraph about shares and copper mines in Africa. 'They never forget you know, elephants,' he continued. 'Still, it's a pity he had to fall off. I'd taken quite a shine to the old fellow by the second lap.' The gentleman's shoulders begun to shake and soon he was giggling uncontrollably as before. 'He landed on a clown of all people, a white faced clown. Sad really, biggest laugh of the clown's career and he was all jam and biscuits.'

Arabella could find nothing to say in reply, so hunted around in her handbag for a sweet and sat back to enjoy the scenery. Occasionally the gentleman would look out from behind his paper as if to start another story. But the giggling would begin again and he would have to return to the more depressing if not humorous news of the day. It was probably for the best as Arabella had spotted the shape of a figure flying in the distance;

one that bobbed over walls and hedgerows as it tried to keep pace with the train. She glimpsed out of the corner of her eye to see if the gentleman had noticed, then returned her gaze to the window. She gasped in surprise, someone in flying goggles and clutching a pink-rinsed 'poodle' was waving frantically at her from outside the carriage and mouthing the word 'door'.

'Heavens-to-Betsy, what on earth is that?' exclaimed the gentleman, but before he could continue Arabella clicked her fingers. She opened the sliding door into the corridor and was met at once by a rush of wind and the figure of Miss Rowena Carp standing in front.

'Now then Arabella, before you begin to tell me off, let me sit down and catch my breath. You can't imagine the morning I've had.' She handed the pink poodle to Arabella and, following her back into the carriage, made room for herself on the seat. 'Is this yours?' she enquired moving a large aspidistra in a majolica bowl off to one side.

'No,' answered Arabella. 'Up until a minute ago it was a rather boring gentleman with a morbid sense of humour. I got the spell a little muddled.'

'Tacky dear, very tacky. Allow me,' and with a click of Rowena's fingers the aspidistra disappeared and a very confused gentleman fell back in his seat.

'Are you alright?' enquired the ladies together, 'You look a little green.'

The gentleman took a few moments to reply, not knowing where he was or why he had this sudden urge to stand in a bucket of water and face the sun. 'Please excuse me, I think this may be my stop,' he spluttered and wiping aphids from his mouth rushed out of the carriage taking his newspaper with him.

Arabella turned to Rowena, but before she could say anything the lady had put her hand up in protest.

'I know what you're going to say, that the flying was foolish. But there was no alternative. I've been hiding from them all morning.'

'Hiding from what?'

'Rats Arabella, giant rats – just as I had seen in the mirror. Terrible slavering beasts they were, and with a thing or two about my undergarments. The horrid creatures were dressed up in my clothes and dancing around the house like it was a gala ball. Urgh! I was glad to burn everything when they had gone.'

'The idea was to burn everything *before* they arrived.'

Rowena stared at her companion through narrowed eyes. 'That's as maybe Miss Perfect, but please don't interrupt. There I was hiding on the ceiling, watching all my Paris gowns being chewed up as bedding when the door slammed open and in strode this man who seemed to know exactly where to look. He stood quite still in the centre of the room, raised his head and stared straight at me. Well, like an idiot I thought I was safe, blending into the plasterwork and cobwebs like a chameleon, but then he began to sniff the air and I suddenly realised those lavender bath crystals you bought me last year were a mistake. Which reminds me, you're getting very cheap in your old age.'

'How do you mean?'

'Those bath crystals dear, scented gravel at best. They don't dissolve. One slip and I'd be ripped to ribbons.'

'Don't exaggerate dear, and get on with the story.'

'Quite…well then, before I realised what had happened this man had picked up a tin of face powder from the dressing table and had flung it straight at the ceiling. Clever trick that, revealing my every outline. 'YOU,' he shouted, then started to lunge at me with his cane.'

'Whatever did you do next?'

'Nothing, but Demetrios here was the perfect hero weren't you,' and in so saying Rowena took the bundle of pink fur from Arabella and clutched it to her bosom. 'Silly little rat-things thought you were a poodle didn't they,' she continued as Demetrios stuck out his forked tongue, breathed a puff of smoke from his nose and gently licked her face. 'Oh, pooh-pooh Demetrios! Your breath!'

'But what happened to the man with the cane?'

'I'm not sure. While this gorgeous pink creature was causing all sorts of havoc in the room, I leapt out of the window and hid in the trees to the back of the house. I returned when it was quiet and the place was empty except for darling Demetrios here, drinking from the lavatory bowl and wagging his tail. There wasn't time to sort out papers to burn so I simply torched the house and flew here as soon as possible. Are you still angry?'

Arabella shook her head and patted Rowena on the hand. It was difficult to stay annoyed with her friend, and she had been so brave.

'Good, because I have a little confession to make, they know where you live and are possibly on this train.'

Forgiveness is a fleeting virtue, and how cruel words can be when spoken in haste. Although it was true Rowena possessed a slight mole on her chin and that in the absence of bleach or a pair of tweezers in the morning she could be described as 'hirsute', only the truly heartless would throw her bananas and clap their hands when she drank tea from a cup.

'How dare you call me a baboon, you sanctimonious old windbag. It wasn't my fault your letter was on the dresser. You shouldn't have written your address at the top, it's pure pretension that's what it is. As if I didn't know where you live. We're in a mess Arabella, and that's all there is to say on the matter. Mindless ape indeed! You're no oil painting yourself, what with those ridiculous false teeth. Stonehenge, that's what I shall call you from now on!'

The two ladies continued their journey in silence, both taking it in turns to stare at the ceiling, floor or out of the window, but never at each other.

'Oh, this is impossible,' complained Rowena after the tension in the carriage became unbearable. 'Are you going to tell me why we're on this train of not? We *are* supposed to be working together after all.'

'I thought it was obvious dear; we're going into hiding. Your little mishap with the mirror is more serious than you seem to think. As soon as we arrive in Grubdale we are to report to the Professor's rooms at once. I sent a telegram earlier this morning so he will be expecting us.'

'Do you think he'll be very cross?'

'I should expect he'll be livid, but if there is anyone who could advise us on what to do then it's him. I suggest we both get some rest, and if anything unpleasant jumps through that door, I shall leave it to you and darling Demetrios there to deal with it. I shall be asleep.' And with that Arabella closed her eyes and feigning slumber snored loud and purposely for one whole hour.

Chapter Two

AN ABUNDANCE OF TWEED

Back in Sodden-on-the-Bog panic had broken out in the cellar beneath Arabella's house. Instead of a small dusty room filled with knotted cobwebs, bottles of wine and stacks of important papers, Vermyn Stench had unearthed an entrance to a cave that stank of reptiles and worse. There were noises too, the slow drip-drop of water, the skittering of bats and now and again the disturbing sound of something large and hungry licking its lips.

Stench was accompanied by three tall rats, Hssk, Skrrt and Chitter, and never had Vermyn a more cowardly bunch under his command. Skewering Krek on the end of his hook may not have helped, but in his defence Vermyn was a stranger to modern theories of man management. He was a disciple of the old school where bottles of mineral water were to be doctored at meetings, not drunk.

The problem with the rats was the light, or rather the lack of a light switch. It was just too dark in the cave, and the overpowering smell of something large and carnivorous didn't help. There could be no turning back. Spleen's orders had been explicit. Vermyn was to seek out members of the Sisterhood, discover their plans then dispose of the interfering women by the most painful means possible. The price of failure was to be found in the Sorcerer's laboratory; a collection of tools and tubes that could unblock the most resistant of drains. Compared with this, even death by 'snake' lost some of its horror.

The same could not be said for the other three. Under the sobering influence of the dark, they had reached a rather different conclusion. When Vermyn twisted the silver claw on top of his cane and a flare of green light shone forth, it was difficult to determine who was the more upset – Skrrt and Chitter on finding a knife at their throats, or Hssk looking down the barrel of a large pistol. That each rat was caught, frozen in the act of killing the other was a surprise to them all, since all three had been intent on assassinating their leader. They remained where they stood, a tangle of weapons and suspicion, each trying to read the other one's thoughts, but with no one admitting their mistake. Only with Stench setting about their heads with his cane were arms lowered and apologies given, and it was a very hesitant and suspicious trio that was finally pushed forward at the end of his boot.

The green light cast large and frightening images on the cave wall. What with the rough limestone surface and the occasional stalagmite thrusting up from beneath, the shadow of the rats holding hands and stepping warily as through a field of open mouse traps would bend and twist into something far more unpleasant. 'Forward,' hissed Vermyn and the rats blunted their knives as they stabbed out at the shadows from fear.

The path through the cave twisted sharply to the left and the unnerving smell grew strong. 'Stop,' Vermyn called. The three rats huddled nervously together as Vermyn placed the glowing cane against a wall and rummaged through the pockets of his coat. He smiled and pulled out a small mechanical device in the shape of a mouse with an ornate key protruding from its back. He placed it gently on the floor and gave it a sharp tap with his foot. 'Ooooh!' crooned the three as a pair of small eyes lit up. 'Aaaah!' they sighed as the mechanical mouse spun around in a circle. But when they pointed and giggled as Vermyn placed a pair of thick steel spectacles over his nose, they knew it was time to shut up. He looked at them disapprovingly. Had they not read the latest manual on field equipment? He twisted the circular frames until each lens clicked into place then pulling back the sleeve of his coat, started to press a series of buttons inlaid at the base of his hook. The mechanical mouse reversed under his feet, then whirred and jerked forward before speeding around the corner and deeper into the cave. The three rats mumbled to each other, impressed. What to Vermyn was a simple tool in the art of espionage was to them a much dreamed of toy and a source of endless pleasure in a chicken hut with a spike attached. They watched with interest as an image of what lay ahead appeared in each lens of Vermyn's ridiculous spectacles. Forget the chickens, they thought, what fun they could have elsewhere. They nudged each other and sniggered.

After a few minutes of Vermyn standing still and tapping furiously at the controls, the mechanical mouse reappeared and was placed safely back in his pocket. The way ahead was clear. There was nothing to be afraid of. He urged them forward with sweeps of his cane and the rats dutifully obeyed.

The walls of the tunnel grew further apart as the cave opened out into a large chamber with a deep, still lake at its centre. There was evidence of recent excavation; an overturned wheelbarrow, a pile of rocks and numerous picks and shovels strewn about the floor. But what interested Vermyn stood far back in the chamber against a roughly hewn crack in the rock wall. It was a wooden chest secured firmly on an iron tripod. A brass funnel stuck out on top, the edges of its mouth beaten flat so that it resembled a large squashed tuba, and from one corner of the chest hung a spiral of twisting flex with a pair of earphones attached. Vermyn examined every detail of the machine, running his claw over the funnel, the wood and the polished brass fittings. He tapped the front of the chest and stood back in surprise as a panel dropped down to reveal a series of switches and dials and a wax cylinder, scratched and broken. He had seen such machines before. It was a 'something-or-other' meter, a recording device. He stretched the earphones over his head and flicked a few of the switches until the machine began to hum, and then twisted the funnel around on top until he found something interesting to listen to. If only he had pointed it towards the ceiling.

From the roof of the chamber high above the unsuspecting rats swung Arabella's pet; a nightmare of a creature that resembled more a giant duvet dipped in grease than anything animal or plant. Not any old duvet, mind you, but one stuffed with tentacles and teeth. It was a cave squid if a name would help, and one that was eager for breakfast. With the sound of a drain rod being pulled too fast from a pipe, the creature let go of its hold and glided silently across the cave to land close by to its prey. It tasted the air with its tongue and shivered with pleasure. At last Arabella had got the message, no more cold beef but fresh, excitable meat. Its jaws opened in readiness and two rows of shark-teeth, like a mangle studded with blades, spun around on their axis showering Skrrt with strips of offal and shreds of corduroy trousers. Before the unfortunate rat could raise the alarm and sign the phrase 'it was nice knowing you', a tentacle shot forth and pulled him off his feet. He tried to squeal but found he had no breath. Neither had he legs and whatever had him grasped around the middle was ripping his nether regions to confetti. 'Leave me some dignity,' was his last pathetic hand signal before being swallowed and filed away for digestion.

The cave squid burped and slid forward even closer, for a single rat was as filling as a cocktail sausage but ever-so-more-ish all the same. Poor Hssk and Chitter, they hardly knew what ate them. With two flicks of a tentacle and the spinning of razor teeth, the first course was over while the main dish of the day remained.

Vermyn Stench stood transfixed, unaware of what had happened but only too aware of what he was hearing through the earphones. Amid the crackle of static he could make out a deep repetitive rumble like the snoring of a giant beast. He replaced the headset, switched off the machine and thought of what next he should do. The clue to the Sisterhood lay behind the crack in the cave wall, but where were his soldiers when there was work to be done? He held his cane aloft and shouted their names, cursing them for their cowardice.

There was a rasping noise to his right. Vermyn turned his head and caught sight of the cave squid, slavering and snarling with its newly found appetite, its mottled, membrane-covered carapace shimmering under the light, and with two cold eyes the size of dinner plates staring back. He edged slowly to the shore of the lake, his steel hook ready to strike, and the cave squid followed, stretching its mouth wide open and licking what was left of the three rats from between its teeth.

The cave squid was cautious, testing its prey with sudden sweeps of its tentacles. There was a mind with this meat and a fury behind those eyes. It lunged at the giant rat's feet then howled in pain as Vermyn struck home with his hook. This was something new to the beast, a meal that fought back. But what was its prey doing now, swimming out to the centre of the lake? There was a smile then a slow slide to the water's edge. This food was exciting, it caused pain - but what if it was choked, if the last bubbles of air could be squeezed from its body? The squid tested the temperature of the lake. Not too cold, it thought, then holding its breath as the water passed over its back, the cave squid began to sink.

Rowena leant back in the comfortable rattan chair and swiped away at the foliage that was trying to sip her whisky and soda. She was seated in the lounge of Grubdale's most prestigious hotel, 'The Alpine Palace', surrounded by potted palms and waiting for her friend Arabella to return from the station. It was a peculiar hotel, apparently favoured by military-looking gentlemen who instead of reading The Times or The Manchester Guardian, were perusing maps of England and circling towns and villages in red crayon. But these were the years immediately before the First World War where a preponderance of German accents in a provincial hotel aroused little suspicion. Admittedly Rowena found the waiter who had brought her drink rather strange. She had asked him for a light for her cigarette and was unprepared for his reply. Tapping his nose with his finger he'd whispered in her ear something not unlike 'the weather in Skegness is very bracing,' then had winked and disappeared around the bar. She sipped at her drink and gazed absent-mindedly at the other female guests in the lounge, trying not to notice Demetrios as he emerged from a particularly bushy plant with a smile on his face. It was pleasing to see the latest autumn fashions on display and surprisingly reassuring to find her green and russet tweeds popular once more.

Arabella sauntered into the lounge with a determined look on her face.

'Over here, dear,' called Rowena.

Arabella sat down next to her friend and ordered a glass of milk stout from a passing waiter. 'Well, thank heaven that's all sorted,' she said. 'We can leave my luggage at the station for a few days until we find somewhere suitable to rent. I do hope you've booked two single rooms.'

'Naturally,' Rowena replied with more severity than was required, for it was an unspoken agreement they would never share the same bedroom again. They had discovered to their cost that one snored like a hippo, and the other had a digestive tract that could poison a cathedral.

'We are to meet the Professor in his rooms at 3 o'clock sharp,' continued Arabella looking at her watch. 'So that allows us plenty of time to freshen up and order something nice to eat.'

The waiter returned with the glass of milk stout and placed it down on the table. Arabella thanked him then glancing at his figure with approval, reached for one of her cigars and asked for a light. The waiter stared at Rowena for a few moments, his mind working overtime, then with a worried look on his face whispered the same strange message into Arabella's ear.

'Skegness?' exclaimed Arabella in surprise. 'What on earth do you mean?'

The waiter hurried away in some alarm while Arabella both blushed and smiled to herself. Such a pleasant, forward young man she thought, seductively brushing her bobbed hair and adjusting her monocle.

'I wish you wouldn't wear that wretched thing,' interrupted Rowena. 'Plain vanity, that's what it is. Why don't you admit you're blind as a bat in both eyes and wear your spectacles?'

'You're only jealous, dear.'

'It's got nothing to do with jealousy. I was thinking of my protection. One glimpse of the sun through that and you'll set my dress on fire.'

'Rowena dear, do shut up and look around the room. Do you notice anything strange? Either our dress is the height of fashion, or the Professor has called a meeting of the Sisterhood.'

Rowena dutifully examined the guests once more and reluctantly came to the same conclusion. Apart from a light dusting of German spies the lounge was filled to the brim with stern, middle-aged ladies in tweeds and sensible shoes all looking crossly at her. She coughed and spluttered into her drink, unhappy with the attention and attempted to shrink from view behind a particularly fine example of a weeping fig.

'It's no use trying to hide, dear. We will have to face them sooner or later.'

'What do you mean 'face them'? We're not on trial, are we?'

'No,' assured Arabella, 'but there will have to be an enquiry. I'm just surprised the Professor has called them together so soon.'

'Harpies, the lot of them!'

'Now that's not being fair, Rowena. They're our colleagues after all.

The Sisterhood is nothing if not united in purpose.'

'Poppycock! I know a certain Miss Trout who'll be more than pleased at seeing me chastised and thrown out of the ranks. She's yet to forgive me for that unfortunate misunderstanding over her budgerigar. I don't care what the old prune says; it was more than delicious and too near a plate of cakes for me to tell the difference. Is she looking this way?'

'Yes.'

'See what I mean, they can't wait to pick over my bones.'

'Now you're being plain silly. Let us put on a brave face and retire with dignity to the dining room. We can order something expensive and think of a suitable excuse over a bottle of wine. They may even have canary on the menu.'

Professor Arbutus Broadbent walked back and forth over the Persian rug in his study, stopping only occasionally to look at his pocket watch. He was not in the best of humour and for good reason. The two ladies were late and from the noise of their conversation as they climbed the steps from the street, they were probably worse for drink as well. He heard the prolonged ringing of the doorbell and the hurried voice of his housekeeper as she ushered the callers into the hall.

'Show them up to my study, Miss Wallace,' he shouted, then adopting a stern and threatening pose behind his desk, he waited for the two ladies to appear. Arabella was the first to put her head round the door and smile. 'You're late,' he boomed. Arabella nodded in agreement. She was about to congratulate the professor on his smart appearance when she was pushed forward into the room by a teetering Rowena holding her 'poodle' and having difficulty in stopping after running up the stairs.

'Sit down the both of you.'

The two ladies smiled back, thinking the request most fine, proper and the very epitome of polite behaviour, but remained standing. The professor pointed to two chairs in the corner of the room and waited patiently as with due formality they were admired, dragged across the carpet, dusted and eventually after much orientation and adjustment in front of his desk, sat upon.

'Miss Wallace,' shouted the professor while staring at the two ladies with half-concealed rage. 'Would you be so kind as to bring a pot of strong, black coffee?'

The housekeeper could be heard muttering some impertinent reply as she walked down the stairs and Arabella and Rowena tut-tutted in disapproval, musing on how difficult it was to find suitable staff. But the professor was not a man to be trifled with. He walked to the sash window and made a great show of sliding it open. 'It smells like a damned brewery in here,' he complained.

The ladies agreed wholeheartedly and looked at the professor with kind, understanding eyes. Who were they to criticise his drinking? Somewhat confused with their concern the professor returned to his desk and flung the afternoon's edition of *The Grubdale Chronicle* into Arabella's lap.

'Stop Press, bottom of the back page, explain yourselves if you will.'

Arabella turned the paper over and with Rowena peering over her shoulder, attempted to focus on the small print. There was a pretty advertisement for beauty soap at the top of the page and a less appealing one for a boiled-down beef drink at the bottom. But no matter how hard they screwed their eyes or how far or close they moved the paper, the required article was a blur of type. They shrugged their shoulders and smiling in all innocence, waited for Professor Broadbent to offer a clue.

'Allow me to summarise,' he fumed, snatching the paper from Arabella and hitting the relevant paragraph with the back of his hand. 'A plague of giant rats in Sodden, a major fire in Frogwallop and the first appearance of a condor this side of the Atlantic, chasing apparently the morning train to Grubdale. Well, ladies, I'm all ears.'

Arabella and Rowena attempted to explain what had happened, and fuelled with strong black coffee poured grudgingly by Miss Wallace, succeeded in recalling most of the important details though not necessarily in the right order, and only after the housekeeper had left the room. The professor interrupted them mid-stream.

'Tell me more about the rats.'

Rowena recounted her escape, but the professor interrupted her again.

'You say this happened in Frogwallop early this morning, but this article refers to a plague of giant rats in Sodden. Are we to assume these creatures are everywhere?'

Rowena looked to Arabella for guidance and described reluctantly how the tall stranger had discovered the letter in her house and her friend's address. At the mention of the tall stranger, Professor Broadbent banged his fist on the desk and asked Rowena to describe his features again.

'Stench!' he shouted, confusing poor Rowena who pleaded that it was not rubbish at all but entirely true.

'No,' continued the professor searching for a file in the top drawer of his desk, 'You don't understand. Here, look at this photograph, one of our agents managed to smuggle this out a few months back.' He threw a faded, silvered piece of paper to Rowena. 'Examine it closely. This is important, Miss Carp. Is that the face of the stranger who attacked you?'

Rowena nodded.

'And is that the face you saw in the mirror?'

Rowena nodded again, and the professor sank back into his chair and held his head in his hands.

'Then it's as I feared.'

Arabella reached out a hand over the desk and patted the poor man's sleeve.

'There, there,' she soothed, 'Things will look better after a bottle of wine. Allow me,' and she proceeded to remove from her jacket a half empty bottle of claret and a dirty glass. Rowena tapped her on the shoulder and held out a large brandy glass. The professor pushed his glass away and rose to his feet.

'This is no time for alcohol ladies; we must keep a clear head.'

'Absolutely' said Arabella and Rowena but not before they had both toasted each other in agreement.

'I shall issue an order effective from today banning the use of the mirrors. We can't risk any further discovery. It means working in isolation, but it may be to our advantage. That creature in the photograph is Vermyn Stench, head of Spleen's secret police. His face in the mirror and the certainty that he has now crossed over can only mean one thing; Spleen knows something of our plans.

Arabella and Rowena looked at each other in dismay. 'The Big Secret?' they asked, and Professor Broadbent nodded slowly. 'Oh dear!' they cried, sobering up immediately as if the housekeeper had thrown a barrel of ice water over them. The *Big Secret* was one of the sacred texts of the Sisterhood, one that had been handed down from generation to generation. It was a collection of writings on the Great Wyrms beginning with their history, their identification and most importantly, an account of their travels. It even had an appendix at the back, not that anyone read it, describing their language and how to sweep up after them; all in all a most impressive publication.

'It's obvious,' continued the professor, 'Spleen has gained control of a wyrmhole. I hope for our sake it's just the one. We must assume it's the same gateway that brought us here and close it at once, but for that we need a Great Wyrm. You wrote in your telegram about certain developments?' Arabella nodded.

'Good, I took the liberty of calling the Sisterhood together. There is a small lecture theatre in the basement of this building. Don't ask me why, most probably an old illegal anatomy school, but those of the Sisterhood that have arrived are waiting for us there.'

The professor walked to his study door and turned the key in the lock. 'Miss Wallace is a good woman but we can't afford to trust anyone. Now ladies, if you would please follow me.' He walked towards the bookcase to the rear of his desk and pulled out a volume of botanical drawings. There was a metallic 'click' and the front of the bookcase disappeared in a shimmering of red light to reveal an ornate lift such as would be seen in only the finest of department stores. He waited for Arabella and Rowena to enter before stepping in behind.

'If I may be so bold as to ask you to keep a firm grasp of your skirts.' He pressed one of four buttons on the side of the wall, and two metal grills slid together, closing the lift entrance to his study.

'Allow me to hold your poodle, Miss Carp.' He pressed the second button and with a whoosh of air the lift fell fast and furious beneath the streets of Grubdale.

George Stubbins poked his head around the open doorway to Arabella's house and looked inside. 'Is anybody there?' he shouted, not wanting a reply, for whoever had broken down the front door had shown a similar disrespect for Arabella's furniture, heavy and oak and smashed into pieces. George struggled with indecision on the doorstep. He could leave well alone, call the police and return to the pub in ignorance, or else investigate the crime scene himself. The opportunity was too good to miss. Here was a rich crop of information to gather, a past life to be revealed in curtains, crockery and bundles of letters. George shouted once more then looking behind for any sign of a guard dog, tiger or worse, stepped over the threshold and entered Arabella's house.

Vermyn Stench pulled himself out of the lake and lay back on the cave floor. He was scratched, chewed and covered from head to tail in thick black ink, but somewhere below swam a more unfortunate creature. He spat out a piece of tentacle and wiped what remained of the beast's eye from the tip of his cane. All things considered, it had been a lucky escape.

He remained as he lay, catching his breath and thinking of what to do. One fact was obvious; he had underestimated the strength of the Sisterhood. Mature ladies of lesser magic aside, a pink devil of a creature had run riot through his troops in Frogwallop and here by the underground lake a cave squid had shredded his companions like a lawnmower through tall grass. If he were to attack in the open, then it would have to be with greater numbers. There was also the question of the recording device, an unexpected development that required careful thought. He was ill-equipped to dig out and investigate the source of the noise, but whatever snored behind the cave wall was obviously important. The more he thought on the matter, the more convinced he was the Sisterhood would return to the cave. All he need do was recruit his force, scatter them through the village and wait like a spider in its web. He smiled to himself confident in his reasoning and getting up from the floor, lit the tip of his cane.

'Is that you Miss Pike?' cried a guilty voice in the distance, 'Are you all right?' It was George Stubbins edging slowly towards Vermyn, using the wall of the cave for support. 'I was just passing your house when I noticed the door kicked in, blimey you look a mess.'

Vermyn quickly extinguished the flame but felt a kindly hand on his shoulder. In those brief seconds of light and with the thick film of ink covering Vermyn's body, George had mistaken his broad outline for Arabella. Before he could strike out with his claw, Vermyn found himself being talked to in a caring, condescending manner and being dragged along the cave tunnel to the cellar of the house.

'Bloody electrics, can't trust the fuses. I miss the old gas myself. Keep a tight hold and we'll be out of here in no time.'

There was a clatter of metal on stone as a collection of cutlery fell from George's pocket. 'I was keeping them safe, can't trust anyone here. I'll pick them up later.'

He steered Vermyn up the cellar steps and into the hall where the light from the open door illuminated the corridor. Vermyn had lost his hat in the fight, and the only recognizable features were his two eyes like white spectacles amongst the black slime and the base of his tail just visible from under the hem of his coat. With years of innocence brought about by a faulty light switch in the bathroom, George continued with the ridiculous assumption that it was Arabella who stood beside him.

'You can't stay here Miss Pike, not until we get you a new door. Let me take you home to get cleaned up. The missus'll pour you a hot bath and lend you some clean clothes.'

So with as little thought to his safety as Caesar tying up his sandals on the Senate steps, George dragged a rather confused but placid Vermyn Stench down the street and into his house.

The small lecture theatre overflowed with ladies in tweed, all waiting for the start of the meeting. Some sat knitting, unconcerned at the delay, while others were more boisterous, eating boiled pig's trotters and throwing the leftover bones at their friends. The doors to the back of the stage slid open and a very dizzy and bedraggled Arabella and Rowena fell out, their skirts all askew from the speed of the lift and with an embarrassed Professor Broadbent standing behind. They ignored the unsisterly comments and with as much dignity as their petticoats would allow, waddled off the stage and collapsed into two empty seats at the front. The professor walked up to the lectern and raised his hands for silence.

'Ladies,' he shouted. 'A little quiet if you please!'

No one took any notice; it had been two years since the Sisterhood had met and there was a considerable amount of gossip to catch up with to say nothing of what may have happened in the lift. Professor Broadbent banged his fist on top of the lectern. 'I call this meeting to order!' he boomed. A pig's trotter hit him on the head. 'Ladies this is serious! Was that you Miss Chubb?'

A group of Sisters waving 'Votes for Women' banners at the back of the auditorium took aim for a second shot.

'I'm warning you, any more of this nonsense and they'll be trouble. Now settle down, please!'

It seemed the bar in the Alpine Palace had done a roaring trade. Someone blew a raspberry.

'Oh, for heaven's sake, don't you realise the danger? We've been discovered by the enemy!'

You could have heard a snowflake fall from the sky and shatter on the pavement, such was the silence in the room.

'Yes, ladies – it's *that* serious, Spleen's agents have crossed over. Even as I speak they hunt us down, and all you can do is act like children.'

At the mention of the Sorcerer's name the audience booed and stamped their feet in disgust. It was a knee-jerk response, their hatred implicit, for Tarantulas Spleen was the reason they were here, exiled from their planet.

Why couldn't they have seen the danger from the start? Their relationship was hardly amicable; Spleen was a court magician and they were a guild of witchery. He would buy their potions and seethe, and they would visit his shows and laugh. Jealousy had set in. True magic was the sole gift of the Sisterhood. Men were unsuited. The winds of magic sat easily with the Sisterhood but in the hands of men became unpredictable and dangerous. Many of the early wizards became burnt and deformed, their life expectancy low, so with time a dichotomy evolved. The Sisterhood used magic while men used science, and by calling himself a magician Spleen had accepted his gifts were sleight of hand, intricate timing and the use of mirrors. He was a master showman but wanted more. It was the eternal drama; a megalomaniac who longed for power or in simplistic terms, it was a male 'thing'. Where was the magic in pulling a rabbit from a hat if a mere woman could yank a fish from a bloated stomach and call it unblocked? And his greatest trick, the sawing of a woman in half was rendered second-rate by the Sisterhood doing exactly the opposite and for half the price around the corner. Jealousy lay heavy with him, slowly twisting his personality, and so the rumours began.

The ladies' potions were nothing but butter, and as for their pills? Ask anyone on the street, they were the back end of a tomcat after the vet had been called in. They were harlots; they danced at midnight in knickers and lipstick; had slept with the devil and seduced the King, and heaven knows what with the Royal Stables. Lock up your sons, keep the tops on your milk bottles and whatever you do, don't play them at cards.

It's surprising what people believe if they read it on a wall and Spleen was a genius in rumour and blame. His campaign was a creeping success, helped mainly by outbreaks of flu and dysentery and the ever present pox, and he wasted no time in blaming it on the guild of witchery. The Sisterhood were being spat at in the streets, and their stalls boycotted. No one wanted their cauliflower foot creams or bottles of purgative, and wasn't it better to be bunged up and sock-rotten than kow-tow to these charlatans? The House of Wyrm began to listen to the poison; it wasn't politic to have 'By Royal Appointment' stamped on the Sisterhood's wares, even if the King was a martyr to the fissures. From now on he would entrust his health to the care of his most favoured advisor, Tarantulas Spleen. Then one morning the people of the city awoke to hear they had a new chancellor, that nice young man in the silks and turban. One year later, with a dagger up his sleeve and the screams of the Royal family still fresh in his ears, Tarantulas Spleen sat down on the throne and saw that it was good.

'How many more times must I ask you to listen?' implored Professor Broadbent. 'It's one thing to boo at his name, but fighting Spleen is quite another. We must plan our actions carefully.'

'How did he discover we were here?' asked a Sister from the audience.

'At last, a sensible question. By careless use of a hand mirror, I'm afraid. Our means of communication are discovered. At the end of this meeting you will hand over all your silver mirrors so they can be destroyed. We can't afford any further breaches in security, which leads me to the reason for our gathering today... progress.'

There was more than a hint of sarcasm in the professor's voice. 'We have been here for ten years and still your reports are few and far between. What progress *have* we made? The only information I seem to receive these days is second hand, scribbled on the back of postcards or printed in the social pages of newspapers. We have become too comfortable; we are here for one purpose only, The Big Secret. Many of you have forgotten this.

'I blame myself; I've been too soft. We have enjoyed freedom and security here, but this is not our purpose. This is not our home. Our home is out there, Vivarium.

'Inactivity is a betrayal of our homeland. Many of you have become successful in new identities, and I congratulate you but remember there is strength in being inconspicuous, of not raising suspicion, of merging into the background. We can't fight our political battles here, and this zeal in which some of you have thrown in your lot with the Suffragettes is of great concern.'

'Stuff and nonsense!' shouted a wild looking Sister wearing a policeman's helmet and a necklace of false teeth. 'Votes for Women and to hell with the rest!'

'Miss Bethesda Chubb!' shouted the professor. 'Remember your place! You are particularly at fault! Being chained to railings and fighting with the local constabulary is one thing, but casting a spell on the Honourable

Crispian Day during his inaugural speech in the House of Commons is quite another. You have served only to draw attention to yourself. Just because the Honourable Mr Day referred to your darling Miss Pankhurst as '*a poisonous trollop,*' is no reason for the poor gentleman to sprout a considerable cleavage and develop a taste for Japanese silks. Your fit of pique has cost the poor man his career. No, I say again to all of you, what about our mission? What has become of Operation Big Secret?'

There was a collective murmur of disquiet in the audience. How dare the professor question their tactics in this way? One of the Sisters put up her hand.

'I have something to say,' she said standing up and addressing the audience.

'Yes? A Miss Haddock is it?'

A few of the ladies giggled behind their hands. Poor Miss Haddock had drawn the short straw when names were being chosen from the Big Book of Fyshes. She ignored her fellow companions and addressed Professor Broadbent directly.

'I am not happy with my assignment,' she said.

'Ooooh-er,' exclaimed the audience in unison.

'This Bishop of Wurms is a *complete* red herring.'

This juxtaposition was too much. Some of the Sisters fell about laughing and threw paper planes in the general direction of a very quiet Miss Herring seated at the front.

'Ladies Please!' shouted Professor Broadbent.

'If I may continue,' Miss Haddock protested, 'I've been sent on a wild goose chase. This title has nothing to do with Dragons or Wyrms at all. To be frank, your information was wrong from the start. There, I've said it. None of us are perfect.'

'And it took you three years to discover this?' asked the professor.

'Well, there was a lot of information to sift through, nice though the trips through Europe were.'

'I doubt you needed three years to come to that conclusion. A weekend in the British library would have yielded the same. You above all others have become comfortable, Miss Haddock. You may enjoy your winters in Switzerland and summers in the South of France, but this is autumn in the North of England and I expect you to work.'

'Well, really!' snapped the socialite and sat down red-faced and fuming. Professor Broadbent looked down a list of names he had taken out of his pocket.

'The Sunderland Chapter,' he read out. 'Where are you? Identify yourselves?'

Three ladies in the middle of the audience raised their hands reluctantly.

LAVENDER AND HADDOCK

'Have you anything to report?'

The three looked at each other then realising they were being singled out for castigation took high umbrage and stared sternly back at the professor. One went so far as to stand up with her hands placed menacingly on her hips.

'Yes,' she replied. 'After *extensive* research we have stumbled across the existence of a Lampton Worm, quite a famous worm in local folklore we believe. We are looking further into the matter and will report more fully at a later date.'

This seemed to impress the other Sisters who, not liking the tone in the professor's voice were muttering a defiant critique on his dress, breath and position in the marriage stakes.

'Very good,' replied Professor Broadbent, 'and have you come to any conclusion?'

'No'

'Then may I provide one. Go to the library. The history of the Lampton Worm is not unknown to me. There is a song of the same name, an old song in which the killing of the beast is described in lurid detail. Perhaps this too is a red herring?'

The spokeswoman for the Sunderland chapter remained standing if somewhat confused, until her friends on either side, not knowing whether she had been congratulated or made a fool of, grasped her skirt and pulled her back into the seat.

'And what news of our gallant Sisters north of the border?' continued the professor looking straight into Rowena's eyes.

'Miss Carp, I believe that means you. Have you not returned recently from the highlands of Scotland? Do you have anything you wish to share?'

Before Arabella could stop her friend, Rowena had sprung to her feet in high dudgeon.

'Actually I do, Mr High-and-Mighty!'

'You tell him girl!' shouted Bethesda Chubb from the back of the room. Rowena smiled in triumph and strode purposefully up to the stage. She turned her back to the professor and addressed the audience with a dramatic sweep of her arm.

'Sisters, I have tremendous news. I have discovered the hiding place of our first Wyrm!'

The lecture theatre erupted into a chorus of applause with the wild Sisters of the Southern Chapter waving their 'Votes for Women' banners and howling like wolves. Rowena bowed gracefully, turned off the lights at the front of the stage and stumbled around in the dark trying to find a switch for the Magic Lantern Projector.

'Please, allow me', spoke Professor Broadbent, and by pushing a large button on the top of his lectern the projector lit slowly up.

'Thank you,' whispered Rowena, 'Now help me put in this slide, it's an only copy so don't drop it.'

The professor obeyed and adjusted the lens at the front until an image of something serpentine came into focus on the screen.

'Behold,' chanted Rowena, 'A Scottish dragon!'

For a few brief moments, the response from the audience was tremendous. The projected image was that of a long neck poking out above the waters of a loch. The fact that a wristwatch was clearly visible and that the 'nose' of the beast resembled five dirty fingernails, seemed lost on all but Arabella and the Professor, until gradually the cheers turned to laughter and then derision.

'What do you mean it's an arm in a pond? I paid good money for that photograph!'

Rowena returned to her seat dejected yet convinced she was in the right. Any fool could see it was a dragon, and why shouldn't the beast want to know the time?

Professor Broadbent was annoyed. 'There is little to laugh at,' he said. 'The enemy is 40 miles away or less. I don't find the fact particularly amusing.' He had made his point, even at the expense of making the Sisterhood seem like a group of giggling school girls. He replaced Rowena's glass slide in the projector with one of his own, and a full-sized image of Vermyn Stench appeared on the screen. The audience shuffled nervously in their seats.

'*Homo rattus*,' he explained hitting the image with the tip of his pointer, 'or to give you its common name, the man-rat, a hideous creation of Tarantulas Spleen. He has taken to the dark arts like a duck to water it would seem, no longer the charlatan. This particular creature goes by the name of Vermyn Stench and is to our present knowledge the head of the Sorcerer's secret police. He was last seen in Frogwallop earlier this morning and may now have travelled to Sodden. We must assume from his actions that he knows the identity of at least two of our Sisterhood, so from henceforth we must be evermore vigilant.'

He changed the slide in the projector.

'It is vital that he discovers nothing of our plans. To this effect, he must be hunted down and destroyed as soon as possible. It will not be easy ladies, as head of the secret police he can call on any number of troops at any time, particularly these.'

The image on the screen changed to that of a pack of rats devouring some unfortunate victim with two large bipedal rats, the size of a ten-year-old child, gnawing at a human foot in the foreground. There was a clatter throughout the lecture hall as a number of uneaten or slightly chewed pig's trotters dropped to the stone floor.

'*Rattus erectus*, or the soldier rat; the main arm of his secret police. Our first task must be to limit their number. To achieve this we must find and close the portal through which they came.'

There was a murmuring of acceptance in the hall with most thinking it a perfectly logical plan, even though a mere man had suggested it.

'But therein lies our problem; this gate is most likely our own wyrmhole, our means of escape. To close it requires a Great Wyrm. To go home requires the same. But I have news, more pleasant than this. I am pleased to say that at least one of our number has made *some* progress. Miss Pike assures me she has evidence of a Great Wyrm sleeping somewhere in this county.'

There was a murmur of excitement from the audience. Arabella Pike was a senior member of the Sisterhood and could be relied upon for her common sense.

'I will now call upon our honoured Sister to deliver her report. Miss Pike, if you would take the stage please.'

The professor walked away from the lectern and dragged to the front of the stage a machine similar to the one Vermyn had discovered in the cave below Arabella's house. Arabella handed him a wax cylinder, which he placed in the recess at the back of the machine.

'Dear Sisters', addressed Arabella to her audience. 'Welcome to my Derbyshire, a county rich in Wyrm history. Let us consider the names: Wormhill, Snake Pass, Lizard Dripping, Wormpit, Wormcast, the River Serpentine, Dragonhole, Adder Hill – all these places have one thing in common...

'They're all bloody horrible,' laughed Miss Chubb. 'Like this weather! Up the Southern Chapter!'

'Bethesda! Please!....No, all these places form a large circle, in the centre of which lies the village of Sodden. It is here where I have concentrated my studies. It has taken many years of work, of secret excavation. I have been lucky; there are many existing mine shafts and underground lakes that have made my search easier. I have used sound recordings throughout and what I am about to play to you today I recorded last month.'

She nodded to the professor, who switched the machine on and immediately a deep, sonorous snoring was heard. Some of the ladies looked around the audience to see who was asleep before realising the noise was coming from out of the funnel on top of the machine.

'It doesn't prove a thing,' laughed Bethesda Chubb again, 'except that Miss Carp was staying at your house'.

'I most certainly was not!' interjected Rowena.

'Sisters please! I recorded these sounds not in my house but *under* it. They come from behind a wall of rock. Listen carefully - are these not the sounds of something large, dare I say gigantic? Is it not written in the 'Big

Secret' that the Great Wyrms are asleep? The most obvious conclusion I leave to you.'

The professor turned the machine around to the front of the stage and moved it closer to the audience. The seats began to vibrate with each successive snore until with a final crackle of white noise, the vibrations proved too much and the wax cylinder shredded into ribbons. After a few minutes of quiet reflection a slow handclap began from the middle of the theatre, then others joined in and soon the whole audience was united in praise for Arabella. If this was indeed the recording of a Great Wyrm then the legends were true, and soon they would be the first people for nearly a thousand years to set eyes on such a beast. Professor Broadbent allowed the applause to die down before stepping back to the lectern.

'We are agreed then. We shall concentrate our search in Sodden. Miss Pike will be in charge of this part of the operation while I shall escort a group of you to Grimspittle Moor to guard the portal. There remains now the question of the prince. Unfortunately, there is no change. He remembers nothing of who he is or where he comes from, but he is safe. At present he is a pupil here at a small boarding school. It is not an exceptional establishment but at least it's close and I can keep him safe. Miss Carp, you are to leave at the end of this week and take up residence there as a teacher.'

'What!' exclaimed Rowena.

'There is a vacancy on the staff, or should I say there will be, and I need you to be near the prince. If the very worst happens then, you must escape with him to Scotland. At all costs, we must not let him fall into the hands of the enemy.'

'Me, a teacher of small boys?'

'Consider it a reprimand, but be kind, he is apparently rather fragile. Now, ladies, there is no time to lose. Your individual orders are contained in these envelopes. When you have collected them and returned your mirrors I ask that you make your way back to your hotel and wait there until I can contact you tomorrow morning. But remember, please be as inconspicuous as possible, our future success depends on it.'

So with the meeting at an end, and with much work to do before the morning, the professor left the theatre and took the lift back to his study.

'Well that's typical,' complained Rowena opening her envelope, 'you lot get the exciting jobs and I'm to teach God-knows-what to a class of soppy boys. No chance of a good fight there'.

'Oh stop complaining, you brought it on yourself, what with the mirror and now that silly photograph. I told you it was rubbish when you showed it me before, but would you listen? Oh no. You were too interested in kilts to realise you were being taken for a fool. And at your age as well, you should be ashamed. Anyhow, we should follow the other Sisters back to the hotel. We can order a nightcap from that nice waiter if he's still on duty.'

LAVENDER AND HADDOCK

And so one by one the Sisterhood left the small lecture theatre by the back door and up the stairs, making their way as inconspicuously as possible along the high street to the Alpine Palace, a seemingly never-ending train of identical red-haired ladies each walking in step and whistling 'LaMarseillaise.'

Chapter Three

SOMETHING NASTY IN THE BATHROOM

There was more than a sense of panic in Sodden. Mrs Stubbins was in severe shock, mumbling gibberish and clutching a crucifix to her breast. What she had presumed to be poor Miss Arabella Pike, covered in oil and with her house not fit to live in was now, after using all the hot water and three bars of expensive soap, a 6ft hairy monster smelling of lavender.

'Bleedin' 'ell, but she's an ugly bugger,' confirmed George looking through the keyhole of the bathroom door as Vermyn bent over to dry himself. He glimpsed something nasty and jumped backwards grabbing the crucifix from his wife. He wasn't sure what he had seen, but whatever it was, was neither human nor decent.

'Quick love, the bedroom!' and clutching his wife's hand he pulled her along the landing, threw her into the back bedroom and locked the door. She stood staring at him with her mouth open, not knowing what to think but fearing the worst.

'That Miss Pike's turned into a rat,' George gasped. 'She must've been bit by one of those big buggers. I've read summat about it in a book. She's a 'were".

'A wee-er?'

'Aye, a 'were".

'Well, I won't have it, George!' Mrs Stubbins cried, somewhat relieved at being left alone and not manhandled onto the bedspread with her toenails caught in the candlewick. 'A giant rat in my bathroom peeing on the floor, it's just not respectable.'

'Be quiet and let me think.'

'No, I will not. I want to know what you're going to do. It's my house and my bathroom…'

'Well I'm not going to get her angry, and that's a fact,' interrupted George. 'You should take a gander at her teeth.' He paused for a moment and stared at his wife. An alarming and uncharitable thought had come to mind, for until then he had not noticed how hairy his wife's arms and legs appeared, bereft as they were of a cardigan and knitted stockings. He edged away slowly and felt for the bedside lamp.

'I don't want you to get mad love, but you weren't bitten this morning were you?'

'What do you mean?'

'It's just that if you were, you could be feeling funny by now, and…'

'George Stubbins, take your hand off that lamp this instant! It's not me you should be frightened of but that thing you've invited into my house.'

'Fair's fair, love. I were only askin''. But before George could offer his wife some cheese from the mousetrap (and clobber her with the lamp if she as much as dribbled), the bathroom door opened and they heard the noise of footsteps on the landing.

'Oh George, she's coming to get us!'

Vermyn was now outside the bedroom, snuffling and sniffing under the door.

'Is that you, Miss Pike?' George asked in the calmest voice he could muster, a mix of gruff landlord and boy soprano on the change. 'We'll be out in a minute. I suppose you'll be wanting some tea?'

'Tea, George? Are you offering that thing tea? Are you mad?'

'Shush love, it's best if we pretend nothing's happened. She might be touchy about her looks and do something nasty.'

The door handle shook as Stench rattled it from the outside and to Mrs Stubbins' surprise George started to suck his forearm and make loud kissing noises.

'George?'

'Pretend we're snogging, love,' he whispered in desperation. 'She might get embarrassed and go away.' But George's plan was flawed in one essential detail. Stench was a stranger to the social niceties of village life. He continued to rattle the handle and slam the door with his shoulder.

'Now, now, Miss Pike, a little privacy if you please!' George shouted. 'Quick, love,' he whispered to his wife, 'open the window, we may have to jump.'

Before Mrs Stubbins could do as her husband suggested, Vermyn Stench broke down the door with a single kick. George clasped his wife close to his bosom and kissed her noisily on the forehead. 'There, finished,' he said, and trying not to stare at the naked monster standing in the doorframe, George dragged his whimpering wife out of the room and asked in a choked voice if Miss Pike would like something to eat. 'I've a nice bit of liver in the kitchen,' he said pushing passed the creature and making for the stairs. 'And maybe a slice of beetroot?' The couple were shuffling as fast as their legs would carry them, but Stench roared in anger and leapt from the top of the landing to land at the base of the stairs. He turned to meet them. Mrs Stubbins screamed and George, running headlong into Stench's solid frame, tried to avert his eyes.

'Please, Miss Pike, think of the neighbours. You'll catch your death of cold if you don't put some clothes on. I'll just nip upstairs and get the wife's dressing gown.' George's ruse failed. Just as he grabbed hold of his wife's hand and attempted to run back up the stairs, Vermyn followed sweeping his steel hook in the air behind their heads.

'I say, what does an old soldier have to do to get served in this place?' It was one of George's customers who tired of waiting for an early pint, had stepped behind the bar and was shouting up the hallway. Stench swerved around to stare at him.

'Is that you George?' the customer asked. 'I can't see from down here.'

'No, it bleedin' aint!' cried the landlord. 'It's Miss Pike and she's in a bit of a mood. Go and get the lads and tell 'em to hurry!'

The customer took sight of the monster spitting and snarling on the stairs and needed no further encouragement. He fled from the pub and could be heard shouting for help at the top of his voice as he ran up the street. Stench turned his attention to George but found the landing empty. He rushed into the bedroom only to see the bulbous head of Mrs Stubbins disappear from behind the window and hear a crash and curse as she landed on her husband. Stench snarled and growled to himself. It was time to escape. What with the petrified customer and now George and his wife creating merry hell outside, he'd soon be trapped. He broke open a wardrobe and searched among the racks of mothballed clothes for something warm to wear, his own tarred and ripped suit still reeking of squid on the bathroom floor. Towards the back of the wardrobe hung George's Sunday uniform, a royal blue suit adorned with silver buttons and braid as befits the post of principal triangle in the village band. Stench squeezed into the jacket and, after tearing a suitable hole in the trousers for his tail, admired himself in the mirror. He completed his outfit with a large overcoat and knitted scarf and, thinking himself every inch a military gentleman, marched downstairs and retrieved his cane from the stand in the hall.

'Take that uniform off at once, Miss Pike!' shouted an aggrieved George through the letterbox, before being dragged away by his wife. 'It's not right,' he moaned. 'A woman in Sodden brass band, it's just not proper.'

Stench crept to the back of the pub and looked out of a small window into the yard. The coast was clear except for George's terrier chewing on a pair of old leather boots left out to dry. He pushed open the back door and, ignoring the half-hearted growls from the dog, made his way over the wall and up through the bracken to the moorland beyond. He walked for an hour through the grass and heather until far below he could see the lights of the village as the evening drew to a close. Nobody had followed, for even the most reckless of the villagers had baulked at George's description of the transformed Miss Pike and, looking out at the full moon from the safety of their houses, had thought it best to wait until the morning before setting out.

A few miles further on and Stench came across a sheltered hollow in the moor. He scraped a wide circle in the soil and stood in its centre, his arms outstretched as a scarecrow on guard. Mouthing the words of an ancient chant he began to spin slowly around, a thin trail of smoke escaping from his snout and hanging in the still air as a spiral. Faster he span, the smoke thickening and rising into the night sky until his whole body was enveloped in a luminous column. With a flash of forked lightning that singed the ground in a circle of sparks, Stench disappeared, leaving behind the faint smell of ozone and the barest hint of lavender and camphor.

'Well I never,' thought a passer-by, or would have done if it were human. For the only witnesses were a group of drowsy sheep, singularly unimpressed and far more concerned in chewing the last drop of sweetness from the autumn heather.

The Alpine Palace hotel in Grubdale was a hotbed of international intrigue. It had come to the attention of the Ministry that many of its guests were a touch too Teutonic, half the kitchen staff partial to a plate of snails and the man in the lift definitely Russian. The public may have been unconcerned, but to those in power these were uncertain times. So where better for the Ministry to install England's most voluptuous double agent, the notorious Frauline Charlie, to pick up on a bit of pillow talk and report back every night from the hotel. It was just a pity she had packed her bags and signed herself into a clinic high up in the Swiss Alps without telling anyone. It was even more of a pity that Miss Arabella Pike and Rowena Carp were staying in the same establishment, and it was downright dangerous that a certain member of the British army had been dressed up as a waiter and sent to the hotel to search out what had happened.

Private Reginald Oldfield was not the best of spies. In the Sudan, he had been at times a palm tree, a camel and on one unfortunate occasion, a speck on the horizon running home to his mother. It was just that he was available. His orders were straightforward. If Frauline Charlie was in the hotel, then she would identify herself by asking for a light, and when prompted with the correct reply would comment on the weather in Skegness. A simple plan but complicated by the recent arrival of a group of mature ladies whose addiction to tobacco was second only to their desire for a dirty weekend at the seaside. It was a confused and battered Private

Oldfield that stumbled down the hotel steps and into the back of a waiting carriage.

'My dear man, you look terrible,' greeted his immediate boss and mentor, Captain Hilary Dashing, and it was all Private Oldfield could do but to nod in reply.

'I mentioned Skegness as I was told,' he explained. 'Then this lady mumbled something in return, and before I knew what was what, she'd dragged me into a broom cupboard.' Private Oldfield paused for breath and wiped the sweat from his brow with what seemed to the captain a large pair of lady's underwear with the Great Wall of China embroidered on the front. 'It was terrible, she was trying to kill me with oriental jiggery-pokery, all pressure points and suffocation if you get my drift, Sir.'

'Quite, quite, Private Oldfield, spare the unnecessary detail.' The captain was uncomfortable with marital horrors and prided himself on cold baths and evenings spent illustrating the New Testament.

'I'm afraid to make my escape I had to hit her with a tin bucket, but not without finding this in her pocket.'

Private Oldfield handed over a crumpled and torn note that the Captain read with obvious interest. It was one of the notes the Professor had written to each of the Sisterhood.

'By Jove, but there's devious work afoot. The Ministry must hear of this at once!' he exclaimed, which by strange coincidence were exactly the same words, although spoken in German and to a German captain, being whispered in a nearby carriage by another bruised and battered waiter to his contact. By virtue of too much drink and the professor's bad handwriting, the stability of Europe was to alter forever. England was now to suspect Germany of developing 'Der Wurm', probably a code word for some despicable war machine capable of drilling under the channel, whilst Germany suspected England of developing 'The Worms', a heinous form of biological warfare once restricted to farmhands or over-friendly cats in Greece. Arabella and Rowena suspected nothing, waking up as they did in two separate broom cupboards, their clothes all creased and with one monster of a headache apiece.

'Did you sleep well dear?' enquired a still-dazed Arabella to her friend later that morning as they sat opposite each other for breakfast.

'Very well, thank you,' replied Rowena holding a raw piece of steak to her eye with one hand and spooning porridge into her mouth with the other. 'And you?'

Arabella tried not to notice the spray of crushed oats and milk that accompanied her question. Even the sight of Demetrios sitting on a chair and wolfing down a fried breakfast seemed to lose its charm. She tucked a linen serviette under her chin and attacked a grapefruit. It was all she could manage. 'The bed was a little hard and I seem to have hit my head on the brass fittings. Other than that I can't complain.'

Rowena stared at Arabella's face briefly and noticed a large red bump on the side of her forehead. 'Well, I suppose I should confess to being clumsy too,' she replied, dodging a squirt of citrus juice that knocked a cockroach off the ceiling and onto Demetrios' plate. 'The reason for this slice of horseflesh pressed to my face is that I stabbed my eye with the toothbrush this morning.'

'It's our age dear,' commiserated Arabella, not believing a word of the story and watching with interest as Demetrios tried in vain to remove with his tongue what seemed like a toffee from his upper palate.

'Absolutely,' agreed Rowena and on the pretext of admiring the décor the two ladies scanned the hotel staff for any sign of their conquests. An unfortunate waiter brushed past Rowena and was delivered of a sharp kick in the back of his leg.

'Terrific news isn't it!' greeted Bethesda Chubb as she joined their table. 'We're to camp out on Grimspittle Moor and be armed with shotguns and real ammunition. Just think of what Mrs Pankhurst could do with those. We could stage a coup and hold Parliament to ransom.'

Arabella slammed her spoon on the table. 'Keep your voice down you idiot. This has nothing to do with that Pankhurst woman and well you know it.'

'Well, hark at Miss Pike. You're not in the Palace now, ordering all of us about and making merry with Royalty. A little armed insurrection is what's needed. Votes for women and chain the men to the sink, that's what I say.'

'Listen to me, Bethesda Chubb. You were a stupid hothead back home, and I see little has changed. Why do you think we risked our lives coming here, to be jeered and spat at once more?'

'I'd like to see someone try. One hint of spit and they'd be on their back.'

'Brave words indeed, it's a pity you weren't like this ten years ago when the Sorcerer sent us into exile.'

At this rebuke the indomitable Miss Chubb fingered her necklace of constabulary dentures and staring at Arabella with obvious hatred, muttered the first words of a spell. Rowena immediately thrust a Cumberland sausage into Bethesda's mouth and pleaded for sanity. 'Calm down, for pity's sake. The last thing we need is a battle of wills. We all know who'll end up the worse off and it won't be Arabella.'

'Mmmmnnnmmm!' raged Bethesda chewing on the sausage and with a 'pop' the half-formed spell dispersed in a burst of purple steam from her ears.

'Arabella and the Professor are right,' Rowena continued. 'Our only concern is to find the Great Wyrms and restore the monarchy. Only a fool would risk that for the sake of a woman who, as far as I know, can't even shuffle a pack of cards let alone conjure with them.'

Bethesda spat out the sausage and turned on Rowena. 'How dare you speak of our Emmeline in such terms!'

'Oh, stop being so tetchy. You're just a silly young thing that's let politics and the smell of carbolic go to your head. Make your peace with Arabella and think yourself lucky you're not a small lump of gristle by now on the side of her plate.'

Arabella and Bethesda shook hands over the table and smiled icily at each other as a field of sparks fell onto the cloth.

'There, all friends again,' soothed Rowena, 'and a good thing too considering the days ahead.'

'Telegram for Miss Carp! Telegram for Miss Carp!'

Rowena looked around the dining room and saw a neatly dressed young man holding up a small envelope and being directed to her table by one of the waiters. She opened the telegram and read through it carefully before shooing the young man away with a sixpenny tip.

'The Professor doesn't waste time. It appears that one of the teaching staff at some school called Grubdale Towers will be taken seriously ill sometime next week. I'm to report for work as soon as it happens. Well, you'd think they'd want an interview. I might not be suitable.'

'What are you to teach, dear?' Arabella asked.

'Horrid little boys, what did you think?'

'No, the subject, silly.'

'Science. Grubdale Towers sounds quite posh really, must be one of those modern, free-thinking establishments.' But, unfortunately for Rowena, nothing could have been further from the truth.

Professor Broadbent met Arabella and those of the Sisterhood chosen to camp out on the moor on the main platform of Grubdale Station. He was holding a battered leather bag and asking a station boy to be careful with a large wooden crate being manhandled into the luggage van.

'Ah, there you are ladies, punctual as ever. Let us hope the railway shows us a similar courtesy. Miss Pike, a word in your ear before we depart.' The professor took hold of Arabella's arm and led her away to a quiet corner of the platform. 'I want you to take this,' he said handing over the leather bag. 'And please be careful. There's a jam jar of explosive, a revolver and some gold sovereigns inside.'

'Explosive?' exclaimed Arabella pushing the bag back into the professor's hands.

'Yes, Miss Pike,' he said forcing Arabella to take hold of the handle. 'You needn't worry. It's quite harmless until you remove the lid and take out the spoon. Now listen, you will need as much help as possible to dig through to the Great Wyrm, let alone wake it up, so the explosive is there to start you off. There's not much, but what there is should be sufficient to breach a hole in the wall. As for the sovereigns, use them to pay the villagers.'

'You mean hush money?'

'Heavens no, how on earth do you think you're going to tunnel through? Recruit some of the villagers to help; they're poor enough not to refuse.'

'But won't they see the Wyrm?'

'Miss Pike, didn't they teach you anything back home? The creature, if it exists at all, will not have eaten a morsel of food for hundreds of years. It will be quite invisible by now, poor thing.'

'Then how will I know where it is?'

'Use your hands and ears. Finding a Great Wyrm won't be a problem, but smuggling the beast out of the village is another matter. I shall need you to contact me then, it is a problem I haven't solved yet.'

'And the revolver?' Arabella asked, opening the bag and taking a tentative look inside. 'What am I supposed to do with that?'

'Ah, yes, the revolver...as I said, the Wyrm hasn't eaten for hundreds of years, it maybe a little peckish when it wakes up.'

'Are you suggesting, Professor, that I go to all this trouble to find the Wyrm then shoot it as it eyes me up for breakfast?'

'No, Miss Pike. It was an attempt at humour. I thought the reason obvious. It's for your own protection. If you happen to bump into Vermyn Stench on your travels, then I fear magic may have little effect.'

'Well, it's a pretty poor plan if you ask me,' Arabella said closing the bag with such a snap that the professor darted for cover. 'And what will you be doing as I blow up half of Sodden, pay its villagers for the privilege and whisper 'good morning' to a half-starved dragon?'

'Don't be flippant,' said the professor reappearing from behind a cast iron pillar. 'I shall be protecting your back on Grimspittle moor along with your Sisters. I'm sorry I can't spare any help, but the destruction of Stench's army comes first, assuming the wyrmhole is their sole means of entry that is.'

'And what if it isn't? Where does that leave me, Professor?'

'Don't worry so. We'll be twenty miles away at most, a petty distance as the ladies fly. If there's no sign of entry, we'll return as fast as we can. That is all I can say. Now come along dear, before the train leaves without us.'

Professor Broadbent hurried Arabella and the other ladies onto the carriage, and after ensuring they were all seated and on their best behaviour, sat down beside Bethesda Chubb and pulled out a newspaper. She nudged him with her elbow and smiled.

'I suppose the guns are in that crate, eh Professor?'

'You suppose correctly.'

'Excellent,' said Bethesda, wringing her hands with glee.

It was early in the afternoon when the train pulled into Frogwallop, and there Arabella said her farewells and walked to the opposite platform. The connecting train to Sodden had yet to arrive, so she sat in the waiting room and looked at the posters on the wall. A few advertised holidays in North Wales, with names too long and vowels too few to pronounce, whilst others boasted of the recuperative effects of being trussed up in a basket and having jets of water squirted at you in Buxton. She shuddered and unwrapped an egg sandwich.

'You can't eat that here,' spoke a tea lady from behind the counter. 'I didn't make it and you didn't buy it. You can have a teacake if you want, they're tuppence.'

'Are you speaking to me?' Arabella asked.

'No one else here.'

'What if I bought a cup of tea, would the Railway allow me to eat my sandwich then?'

'I suppose so, but only if you sit near the door. I can smell that sandwich a mile off.'

'Then I shall have a cup of tea. Two sugars and a slice of lemon if you please.'

'You can have a whole bleedin' pineapple if you want, but seeing I've no basket of fruit on the counter, how does milk suit?'

'Milk will be fine, thank you.'

The tea lady poured out a cup and sloshed a drop or two of milk into it from an enamel jug.

'Let's call it cream, the milks off,' she said, sniffing the contents. She brought the drink over to Arabella and stood over her, having nothing else better to do.

'Travelling far then? You're too late for the London train.'

'Only to Sodden, I've been away on business.'

'Sodden is it? Brrr! Cold, wet and full of moor-peeps.'

Arabella took a sip of tea then pushed the cup away.

'You know what I mean, hill folk. They peep up from behind walls when you pass by in the bus. They're not very bright. You should hear their latest – they think there's a monster in Sodden. You have to laugh.'

Arabella sat up straight at this news.

LAVENDER AND HADDOCK

'A monster? What do you mean?'

'Oh, just some moor-peep nonsense. More likely a cow. They don't get many cows up there. That'll be thruppence for the tea and cream.'

'Here's a penny, and be glad of the change.' Arabella threw the coin on the table and, noticing her train pulling into the station, picked up the leather bag and strode off to the platform. A woman, not looking where she was going, knocked her to the ground.

'I'm so sorry,' she apologised and offered Arabella her hand.

'You needn't bother!' snapped Arabella, 'just watch where you put your feet.'

The woman stared at Arabella in horror, dropped her shopping on the floor and ran off in the opposite direction, screaming.

'Moor-peeps, what did I tell you,' quipped the tea lady, but Arabella wasn't listening. She had remembered the delicate contents of the leather bag and was fighting the natural instinct to throw it away and run for her life. Her hands shook as they pulled the clasps apart. Thankfully the jam jar was intact.

'Are you alright?' the tea lady enquired. 'You look shook up. Nothing broken, I hope?'

Arabella wiped the sweat from her brow and closed the bag.

'No, I'm fine thank you. Just a little flustered, that's all.' She dusted herself down and climbed on board the carriage.

'It comes from living so high up,' shouted the tea lady.

'What does?'

'Their peculiar behaviour, lack of oxygen, they say.'

However peculiar the woman on the platform had been, it was mere quaintness when compared with the passengers on the train. Arabella had managed to find a compartment for herself and was dozing and dreaming of happier days when she was aware of a shadow from outside the corridor. She opened one eye, wiped a string of dribble off her chin and looked to her left. A small group of passengers had their faces pressed up against the glass of the compartment door and were staring at her in horror. Arabella looked to her right, to make sure no hideous monster was trying to break through the window but saw the usual blur of nettles and hawthorn as the train sped through a cutting. She even checked her face in the mirror, yet found herself as attractive as ever and not at all a subject for scrutiny. 'It's rude to stare!' she complained, but instead of receiving an apology, two of the group fainted, one made the sign of the cross, and another ran down the corridor whimpering like a scalded dog. 'What is it?' she shouted through the closed door. 'What's wrong with you all?'

The man who had made the sign of the cross reached into his jacket and pulled out a tattered and much-used Bible. He held it tight to his heart and with his eyes closed, adopted the manner of an early Christian in the

Coliseum, swaying gently and trying his hardest not to look like a tin of cat food. Arabella slid the compartment door open and asked very politely if the gentleman was quite mad.

'Be gone with you, evil spirit!' he preached. 'Leave the body of this innocent woman.'

'You are not by any chance referring to me?' interrupted Arabella, 'because if you are, then I should tell you now, I find it in very poor taste.' Before the man could reply, let alone sprinkle Arabella with holy water, the train came to a screeching halt and sent the unfortunate gentleman head-over-heels to the back of the carriage.

'What's the problem now, not a sheep on the track, surely?' thought Arabella and stepped into the corridor to investigate. The two passengers who had fainted were now wide awake and crawling as fast as they could away from her. Arabella ignored them and, stepping over their cowering bodies, opened the connecting door to the next carriage and walked through. There was no one there, let alone a guard, and through the carriage window she could see the driver and fireman running away along the track. Whatever had scared them must be horrible indeed, and for the first time that afternoon Arabella considered the possibility that Vermyn Stench was somewhere on the train. Hadn't the woman on the platform seen something terrible? A brief glimpse of Stench's tail through the window could have explained the passengers' behaviour. Perhaps he was on the roof?

Arabella drew out her revolver and decided to investigate. Carefully opening the door that led outside, she stepped down from the carriage and walked slowly to the front of the train. She pulled herself up on the footplate and climbed on top of the stack of coal at the back. She could see nothing on the roof but recognised the surrounding scenery. The train had stopped only a mile outside of Sodden. Perhaps Stench had jumped down and was waiting for her below. Just to make sure, Arabella scrambled to the ground and checked each side of the train and under each carriage until all that remained was a final search inside. There was nothing, there was no one there, and Arabella chided herself for wasting time. Now she had to walk the mile along the track and hope that no one lay in wait for her ahead.

Chapter Four

THE VICAR'S GREAT PLAN

George Stubbins had had a fitful night's sleep in the spare room at the vicarage. His dreams were full of hairy beasts breaking into the pub cellar and drinking his stocks dry, and to make matters worse, the vicar had kept him awake till the early hours of the morning with tales of possession, poltergeists and cats that waited under the bed for the first sign of a foot. If anything George should have been delighted with the vicar's response; he had proven both an eager audience and willing believer in the evening's events. Instead of simply laughing at George's story and running off to the kitchen to hide the cutlery, the vicar had been transformed into a veritable witch-finder general, spouting fury and retribution with each sip of his favourite port.

'It's no good love,' George told his wife on waking up all covered in sweat. 'Beast or no beast, we should never have left the pub. Anyone could have broken in, let alone that Miss Pike rummaging through our wardrobe. First thing we do today is see about reclaiming our property.'

'But what if she's still there George? You saw the sight of her. One sweep of that tail and I'll be nothing but a grieving widow in Frogwallop, spending all your money.'

'Then you'll be as poor as a church mouse. That last trip to Blackpool did for me.

'Now listen, love, I've been thinking. Miss Pike is a were-rat; we'll be safe by now. It's daylight outside, and she should be back to her old peculiar self.'

'But what happens when it gets dark George, tell me that? She'll go all ugly on us, and nobody will be safe. The whole village is in danger if she's allowed to roam free. I agree with the vicar, we should catch her and take her to the police. I won't have her in my bathroom, not a second time.'

George thought over this advice while pulling on his trousers.

'And just how are we going to do that?' he asked. 'The vicar was full of drink last night, lots of talk but short on action. It's not like we can creep up behind Miss Pike and bump her on the head.'

'I don't see why not, that's what you were going to do to me last night with the bedside lamp. Why should she be any different?'

There was a knock on the door. It was the vicar still animated from the night before.

'Rise and shine my warriors, it's almost noon and there's much to do. I've warned the village to be on the alert, so hurry along. There's kippers and strong tea on the table, and I like my food hot.'

'I don't like kippers,' whispered Mrs Stubbins, 'they taste like fish. Can't we ask him for porridge?'

'So, Mr Stubbins', said the vicar after finishing his meal and wiping his mouth with the edge of the table cloth, 'ready to do battle?'

'That depends; I'm not a violent person by nature.'

'Nonsense Mr Stubbins, the blood is up and the hunt is on. This is no time for half-measures. We must rid the parish of that ungodly woman once and for all. The times I've suffered her infuriating cigar smoke, coddled logic and jars of chutney. She's pure poison and an enemy of the cloth.'

'What I mean, Vicar, is it depends on what I have to do. You must admit she's a bit on the large side.'

'Yet what of David and Goliath? Think on that, Mr Stubbins. Remember your Old Testament; size is unimportant if one's heart is true. We must chivvy her out of your pub like a ferret, and you must be as the brave shepherd boy with the sling.'

'I shall need something more than a sling, Vicar. It'll be a big pebble that brings Miss Pike to the ground.'

'Pish and tush, it's all a question of physics and a good eye. Look at me, I'm not known as the 'Terror of the Belfry' for nothing. There are no cleaner bells or bird-less spires in the whole of Christendom. My larder is replete with plump pigeon and smoked bat.'

Mrs Stubbins felt suddenly ill and crammed a piece of dry toast in her mouth.

'Enough of this faint hearted talk. Do you think I would lead you to battle unprepared? Shame on you Mr Stubbins, while you were both sleeping, I was hard at work organising our campaign. Come now, get off your chair, it's time to dress the warrior!'

George not so much stood up as was dragged to his feet.

'We shall start with your suit of armour,' and courtesy of the vicar's sporting past, George found himself being wrapped one limb at a time in a collection of cricket pads and cushions. Then came his trusty 'sword', an

Excalibur of a golf club that due to its tendency to lose the game whenever wielded with flourish, had been relegated to chief poker amongst the fire irons.

'A little tap to the head will be sufficient. Take my word for it. In my last game, I was banned from the clubhouse and branded a hazard in the next county.'

George swung the club around to get the feel of the weapon.

'Ah,' purred the vicar, 'a veritable champion in pose. Perhaps we should return to the question of your membership of the golf club at some later date.'

George frowned at the vicar and lowered his weapon. Some things were better left unsaid, especially if they referred to the effect of a night on the beer and pickles when bending over for a difficult putt on the seventh.

'Don't you think this may be a bit over the top?' asked George in all honesty. 'We only need to disarm her, not hit her for six over the church spire.'

'Quite so my man,' answered the vicar dragging a large roll of dusty string netting from out of a cupboard. 'But have I not thought of everything? All you need do is wave the golf club round, and as soon as she runs out of the door I shall catch her like a herring with this.'

He unfurled the netting on the floor and stood back with admiration, for this was a cherished possession of his youth, a memento of happier days as a student in Cambridge.

'Tennis,' he sighed, 'now there is a game. You may not think it Mr Stubbins, but I was once considered something of a wizard with a racket and ball, thwacking the old Bishop around the court on a warm summer's evening, God rest his soul.' He pulled George suddenly towards him and whispered in his ear.

"Treachery' the Dean called it, 'Nothing less than murder'. But tell me this - how was I to know about his Grace's weak heart, or the Dean spooning heaps of sugar into the Bishop's tea? Oh no, I knew who the traitor was, and haven't I suffered for it ever since?'

George pulled himself away from the vicar's grasp; the man was quite mad or else still drunk on port.

'Come now Mr Stubbins, it's not me you should be afraid of, think of the enemy.' He patted George reassuringly on the shoulder. 'Are you fit?' he asked.

George nodded in reply.

'Excellent, then lead the way brave soul, your good wife and I will follow close behind with the net.'

So, at the very same time that Arabella was waving goodbye to her companions on Frogwallop Station, the brave trio left the vicarage and advanced with solemn purpose towards the front of the pub.

'I don't wish to be rude Vicar, but if you wouldn't mind stepping back a few paces. It's difficult walking in these cricket pads as it is without having you kicking my heels from behind.'

'Sorry dear chap, safety in numbers and all that.'

The vicar and Mrs Stubbins backed away while George strode up to the front step, lowered himself to his knees and peered through the letterbox.

'Well?' asked his wife. 'Is there anyone there?'

'Shush love I'm trying to listen.'

He rattled the cover and shouted 'Coo-ee!' and on hearing no reply, pushed the door open and put his head around to see.

'Get out of it, you daft bugger!' he hissed as his nose suddenly met the cold, wet same of his terrier, barking and wagging his tail in greeting. 'Phwoar, but your breath smells, bread and milk for you from now on.' He pushed the dog aside and stood up on his feet, glad that the bar was empty. Like a blind man in a china shop during the January Sales, George waddled across the room with the club held out in front and made for the stairs. He faulted on the first step, the image of Miss Pike rabid and gnashing her teeth was still fresh in his mind, and no matter how hard he coaxed his legs forward, they remained where they were, rooted to the spot and shaking from fear. 'Come on George,' he chided himself, 'pull yourself together.' He felt a nudge on his shin and looked down to find the terrier lying on his foot and looking up at him out of sheer devotion. 'Good boy Scutt,' he said affectionately and bent down to pat the dog's head.

An idea came to him, simple in its cowardice. 'Rats!' he hissed pointing to the landing, 'rats boy, rats!' and, as though the dog had sat unwisely down on a nest of ants, Scutt jumped into the air and ran around his master's feet yapping and snapping with excitement.

'Not down here you stupid mutt, up there!'

Scutt raced up the stairs and disappeared into one of the bedrooms. There was a crash and the sound of breaking glass, then Scutt sprinted off into the next room.

'Mind the furniture!' George shouted, but Scutt was uncontrollable, a slave to the rush of hormones coursing through his body, his world a red mist of rodent's tails poking out from behind curtains and, alas for Mrs Stubbins, each china vase as well.

'Oh no' thought George, 'Miss Pike *is* here.' From the noise Scutt was making it was obvious that the terrier had discovered something; there was snapping and growling, and the sound of elastic being stretched.

'That's it Scutt!' shouted George walking backwards to the front door. 'Let her have it, chase her down to me!' The cowardly landlord had no intention of remaining in the house and as soon as his back bumped into the handle of the door, he pulled it quickly towards him and slipped outside.

'Get ready you two,' George cried as he stumbled down the front steps. 'Hold that net taught!'

Mrs Stubbins and the vicar prepared themselves for action, each running to the opposite side of the street and stretching out the tennis net as far as it would go. A small group of villagers cheered them on, waving cudgels and handbags in the air and, spurred on by the wild ranting of the vicar, proclaimed how they had never liked the peculiar Miss Pike in the first place.

'A little silence please,' implored the vicar. 'We don't want to give the game away.'

An almighty 'snap' was heard from inside the pub followed by a yelp and the sound of something substantial hitting the floor. The growling and yapping continued until, like a zephyr of fur and cotton, Scutt tumbled out of the pub shaking and ripping a pair of George's best winter long johns. The villagers began to point and laugh, and Mrs Stubbins hid her head in shame. George's combinations were a challenge to the dolly tub and a dead ringer for the Shroud of Turin. The vicar dropped his end of the net and walked across to Mrs Stubbins. He placed a comforting hand on her shoulder and addressed the villagers.

'No laughter, please! Show some charity if you will.'

Some of the villagers obeyed while those who boasted the latest starch and soda crystals continued to chuckle and criticise the laundry.

'Well Mr Stubbins, it seems your pub is empty. I suggest we search the surrounding area. Can we rely on that dog of yours? Has it a nose for something other than underwear?'

'Scutt, you mean? He's the best ratter this side of the moor. He was just off colour yesterday.'

'Then the operation is in your hands. I shall instruct the villagers in the art of pursuit while you see to your dog. I suggest you get out of those cricket pads. I can't see you marching across the moor in them, useful though they are.'

So George and his wife, glad to redeem themselves with the village sprang into action dragging the still snarling Scutt inside the pub by the collar. While Mrs Stubbins wrestled with the dog for the underwear, George set about unbuckling the cricket pads and finding something in the house that could lead Scutt to the scent. He came across Stench's clothes still smelling of squid in the bathroom, but when he wrapped these around the dog's face and whispered 'Go on boy, search her out!', Scutt's eyes watered and his legs began to tremble.

'What about the soap?' suggested Mrs Stubbins. 'From the number of bars that woman used she must be a walking perfumery.' So poor Scutt had his face thrust into a bag of bathroom toiletries and still dizzy from the fumes, was carried outside by his proud master. George placed the confused terrier down and beckoned the villagers to stand aside.

'Give 'im room, let the poor dog breathe, he's trying to find the trail.' And so Scutt was, for after a few shaky moments where the crowd thought the dog asthmatic or about to be spectacularly ill, the plucky terrier pricked up his ears and began running around the road, his nose sniffing the ground and his tail wagging twenty to the dozen.

Alas for Mrs Stubbins, it seemed that lavender was a common commodity in the village. After a few circuits of the crowd, Scutt sat down in front of a young farmer and sniffed and barked at the man's trousers. George cast a suspicious glance at his wife. The young lad was single and a stranger to posh soaps. Either Scutt was an idiot or his wife was a trollop.

'I'll speak to you later, you...you Jezebel', he mouthed then walked up to the young farmer, stared at him sternly and snatched Scutt up into his arms.

'Don't mind me, Mr Stubbins,' said the lad in all honesty, 'I often slip your old dog a sausage or two.' Before the lad could explain further, George had knocked him to the ground with a single punch. The vicar ran over and held George back.

'Gentlemen, please!' he cried. 'Not in front of the ladies, stop this nonsense at once!' He helped the young lad from the floor then turned towards George. 'Mr Stubbins, I haven't a clue what made you strike the poor boy, but whatever the reason I want you both to shake hands. I have better things to do than referee a boxing match.'

'Hang on a minute Vicar,' protested the young lad rubbing his chin and sitting down again, 'I'm not getting up before I get an apology. All I mentioned was giving the dog a bit of food. That's why he's barking at me; he thinks it's dinner time.'

George was confused; that was not what the young lad had said at all. He thought on the matter further until the embarrassing truth hit him on the back of the head along with a dinner plate thrown by his wife. He had jumped headfirst and careless to the wrong conclusion, but what could he say by way of explanation? He rubbed the bump on his head and tried to ignore the sound of the pub door slamming and the curses of his wife as she stormed off to her mother.

'Well Mr Stubbins,' said the vicar. 'The boy has a point. You owe him an explanation.'

Poor George could think of nothing to say other than admitting he was a fool. A figure at the back of the crowd hobbled forward on a walking stick saving George from further misunderstanding. It was one of his regular customers. The man stumbled into George's arms and hugged him close.

'By heavens, you're alive!' he slurred, spouting cheap whiskey fumes and spittle into George's face. 'Thank God, I thought your number was up!' He kissed the landlord on the side of the cheek, overtaken with the emotion of the moment, and happened to glance at the young lad, still sitting on the ground. He assessed the situation and chuckled. 'Blimey George, what's the young rascal done now, run off with your missus?' For some reason the man found this statement hilarious and burst out into peals of drunken laughter, and attempting to look useful he rolled up the sleeves of his coat and advanced on the boy.

'I'll take a swipe at the young whippersnapper myself.'

'You'll do no such thing Bill Hicken,' interrupted the vicar. 'Just look at the state of you, not half past twelve and you're as high as a kite.'

'And so would you be, if you'd seen what I did last night. A creature from the bog it was, come to haunt us all. Tell 'em George.'

'I don't need to Bill; the entire village knows about the beast. We're going to hunt her down and give her up to the police.'

'A posse eh? Well, count me in.' Bill puffed up his chest like a strutting pigeon in the first throws of spring passion, and forgetting his cowardice from the night before, thrust his walking stick under his arm and saluted the Reverend Cross.

'Allow me to be of service, Sergeant William Hicken, retired, 1st Grubdale Rifles at your command, Sir!' He teetered on his feet and if it were not for George holding him up from behind would have fallen beside the unfortunate youth on the floor.

'There's no need to salute,' said the vicar, 'We're all equal in the eyes of God.'

'Glad to hear it, so what are we waiting for?'

'We are waiting for no one. Mr Stubbins was about to lead the way down the street, assuming that his terrier could pick up the scent.'

Bill Hicken turned sharply around and attempted to focus on George's face.

'Permit me to speak George, but you're making a big mistake. I saw the brute escaping up the hill behind the pub. We'll get nowhere standing here. I have a better idea; let Old Sherlock take the front. That dog of yours couldn't find his tail in a chase.'

At the mention of Old Sherlock some of the women in the crowd shivered while George, the credibility of his beloved terrier being called into question, pooh-poohed the idea and placed Scutt on the ground before him.

'Are you saying my dog isn't up to the job?'

'In a nutshell, dear George. Allow me to illustrate.' George looked on unimpressed as Bill searched inside his coat and, to the further horror of the ladies in the crowd, deep within the lining of his trousers. After a few minutes of intense concentration punctuated with the occasional grimace and wobble as he struggled with whatever was down below, Bill Hicken removed Old Sherlock from the fabric of his clothes and waved it aloft like a decrepit Statue of Liberty signalling with her torch.

The crowd backed away to form a wide open circle, for Old Sherlock was a legend in the village; the fattest and most flea-bitten ferret that ever had the misfortune of running up a trouser leg. While no one could accuse the animal of being vicious, it's hunting instincts forgotten in a haze of eggnog and brown ale, the ferret's affectionate wandering when loose in the pub was cause for concern if not a pulling up of the gang planks. Many a quiet game of dominoes had been ruined by the wide-eyed stare and frantic tap dance of someone intimately interfered with. It was fortunate that Bill had recently taken to tying the ferret to his trouser belt by a long piece of string. Not only did this make for a more pleasant evening, but enabled Bill to be pulled home when full to the brim and spilling with gargle.

Scutt took one look at the mewing ferret in Bill's hand and decided to retire with some dignity, his tail tucked securely between his legs. Old Sherlock's affections weren't limited to corduroy and trouser lint.

'Sorry George,' chuckled Bill placing the ferret on the floor, 'it seems your dog has made his mind up for you.' As soon as these words had left Bill's lips Old Sherlock set off scampering after the terrier, pulling his owner off balance and sending him teetering forward on his toes.

'Here we go everyone,' shouted the vicar. 'It looks as though we have the scent.' And so the gang of villagers ran after the stumbling Bill Hicken, past the side of the pub and up into the hills beyond.

'Blimey, I didn't know the old man had it in him,' said George trying to catch his breath. Bill was a few yards ahead, still tripping and crawling through the heather with his beloved ferret pulling on the string.

'It's no good, I'm going to have to lie down and rest, I'm not used to this pace.'

The vicar agreed wholeheartedly with his friend and called the group to a halt.

'Come on Bill,' he shouted in between gasps. 'There's little point in killing ourselves. Have a heart will you and stop for five minutes while we catch our breath. It'll make no difference to the chase.'

Bill seemed to have heard, for he clutched at his chest and fell forward, the only indication of his presence being the outline of the ferret repeatedly jumping into the air.

'Phew,' exclaimed George lying back in the heather, 'I thought Bill would never stop, and him with the dodgy leg. I tell you one thing Vicar, we can all scoff at his bachelor ways, but he certainly thrives on that diet of his. Fish and chips and a bottle of scotch, I'll tell the missus that's what I want from now on. None of this fresh fruit and toasted cereal malarkey she's been trying to poison me with. Give me something filling and alcoholic.'

LAVENDER AND HADDOCK

'I know exactly what you mean,' agreed the vicar dropping the rolled up tennis net and sitting down next to him. 'My house keeper insists I eat sour curds of a morning with my kippers. Not a pleasant diet. Only last Sunday I had to cut short my sermon by a full twenty minutes.'

'Curds? I wouldn't feed them to a dog.'

'I'm glad to hear it.'

'Of course I blame it on that new tea shop in town. I can't stand the place, but the missus swears by it. 'The Hedgerow' I think it's called, and you wouldn't believe the muck they serve up. Fruit teas, vegetable drinks and cakes full of twigs.'

'Sounds abominable.'

'It is Vicar, it is. The missus is never the same after visiting the place, unnaturally active with bits of greenery trapped between her teeth. A horrible sight, I can tell you. I lock myself away in the shed till the effects wear off.'

'You poor man, I shall forbid the housekeeper from setting foot in the place.'

They lay back in the heather, staring up at the sky and musing on the absurd ways of the world when some of the villagers began shouting and pointing at the railway line in the distance.

'Get up Mr Stubbins; we have sight of the fox. Tally ho chaps, tally ho! Well done that man there!'

George sat up and looked where the crowd were pointing. Sure enough, the unmistakable figure of Miss Pike could be seen entering the last tunnel before the village station.

'If we hurry we should make the exit before she reappears, come on Mr Stubbins, we have no time to lose. We can throw the net over her from the top of the cutting.'

The gang of villagers whooped and cheered with delight as they set about running, sliding and rolling down the hillside, leaving only poor Bill Hicken behind; a broken, winded man fearing the worst from the pains in his chest.

Arabella struck her last match and peered into the entrance of the tunnel, but for the third time a gust of wind extinguished the flame before she could make out what lay ahead. Perhaps a spell was needed. She was safe from spying eyes and decided that no possible harm could come from a teeny bit of magic. It would be good to exercise her brain for some spells were as fragile as gossamer and easily forgotten. *'The Flaming Ball of Geshenck,'* thought Arabella, an easy spell to start with but if only she could remember the words. No, this was being silly. Her head was muddled from the night before. She mumbled a phrase or two, clicked her fingers and at once her stockings caught alight. 'Blast!' she swore and cast what she believed to be the *'Damp Effluvium of Belge'* only to be drenched by a fountain of ice-cold water. How annoying, a senior member of the Sisterhood fumbling her spells like a novice. What would her companions think? She tried to focus on creating the fireball for a second time and stumbled upon the necessary order of words to use. There was a flash of sparks and a sphere the size of a football appeared over Arabella's head and glowed white hot. 'Oh dear,' she groaned as the interior of the tunnel lit up, 'hardly what I'd call inviting.'

The damp, soot and oil had stained every inch of brickwork black, and between each sleeper were puddles of greasy water. Arabella gazed down at her clean and polished shoes and thought better of walking the length of the tunnel. There were standards to be maintained, and taking good care of her sensible footwear was high on the list. She cast a simple levitation spell and floated two feet from the floor then, pointing ahead with her outstretched arm, dropped like a stone into the nearest puddle.

This was more than mere coincidence. Three spells had gone askew, one after the other. Arabella remembered Professor Broadbent's words to her that morning. 'I fear your magic may have little effect.' Is this what he'd meant, and hadn't Vermyn Stench seen through Rowena's spell of invisibility the day before? Arabella stepped out of the water and withdrew her revolver. There were two possibilities, either she was all fingers and thumbs or else Stench was close by and interfering with her flow of magic. At least the fireball hung intact, illuminating the tunnel with its brilliant light. There could be no possibility of surprise, no rat's claw grabbing her from behind, but she could hardly remain where she was. She needed the help of the village, so gathering her courage in a single scream, Arabella fired her revolver and sprinted as fast as she could to the other end of the tunnel.

'Got her!' shouted the vicar as Arabella ran headlong into the tennis net. 'Haul away men, let's pull our little fishy in.' Arabella was anything but little. It took a line of villagers nine strong to huff and puff and drag the poor lady up the side of the embankment.

'I'm sorry, Miss Pike,' the vicar said as he wrapped her up in a tight bundle. 'It's for your own good, you're not well.'

Arabella could do nothing. Her mouth was stuffed with an old handkerchief, and her arms bound securely behind her back.

'You'll laugh about it in the morning, really you will. It's just tonight we are worried about. There's a full moon, and someone may get hurt. That's why I've arranged for you to stay in the church crypt. You can bang about there to your heart's content.'

George was feeling guilty; the villagers were making heavy work of carrying Arabella down the hill and had dropped her a number of times in the heather. He pulled the vicar to one side, unsure of the plan. 'We can't keep her locked up indefinitely,' he said. 'What shall we do in the morning?'

'Honestly, George, ye of little faith. We'll simply photograph her tonight as she starts to 'change'. I'm sure that's all the evidence the police will need, and by this time tomorrow Miss Pike will no longer be a problem. Now why don't you be a good man and run on ahead to the pub, I think we all deserve a drink after today, don't you?'

George felt every inch a traitor as he made his way down the hillside. It was sad to have seen Miss Pike trussed up as game, but in his heart he knew it was for the best, as long as the police understood. What if the vicar was as hopeless at photography as he was at golf? Where would the conspirators be then? He tried not to think on the matter and cheered himself up by putting an extra penny on a pint and thruppence on a tot of whisky, only for the night though, just to see him nicely in profit.

George heard singing and laughter coming from his pub. Well, he thought, good news at last. The missus must be home. She may have a hot temper and a habit of visiting her mother's, but at least she knows what side her bread is buttered. 'Hello love, I'm back,' he shouted grabbing an apron from the kitchen door as he walked through to the bar. Mrs Stubbins had her back to him and was filling glass after glass with beer. 'That's it, love; work away, time's money. Now then gentlemen, it's not often we get such a good house this early in the evening. Who's next?'

Mrs Stubbins burst into tears and threw a pint pot at her husband. 'You silly fool, George Stubbins, open your eyes, can't you!'

George was about to say something uncharitable when Vermyn Stench slammed an empty beer glass down on the counter and along with his other rat-men, demanded a refill.

Chapter Five

A RAT IN A TRAP

To say that Bill Hicken was unconcerned as he lay face down in the heather would be to describe crochet as the sport of kings or chewing tripe on a wet afternoon a pleasant way to attract the ladies. He had arrived at a crossroads in his life, that singular moment when on stepping from a shower a gentleman catches his reflection, full length in the mirror. It is then that the fates conspire to whisper possibilities; to live like a gerbil or else gamble with the devil and take a hammer to the glass. Bill had weighed up the odds and arrived at a momentous decision. He would put his ferret on a diet. Old Sherlock was too big and too strong to be tied to his trouser belt. It was a question of balance, for Bill's physique was not what it was, once strapped with sinew and with a stomach like an egg box. After years of Scotch whiskey and greasy fish suppers, his muscles were so wasted they would sing in the wind. Take the day's outing, while his ferret had romped and pranced uphill, Bill had been propelled by a series of jerks from one clump of heather to another, not unlike the sensation of having your braces caught in a tram door with too many stops on the high street.

Bill managed with an effort to sit up and waited for his heartbeat to return to normal. He could see the group of villagers in the distance carrying what seemed like a small whale wrapped up in a string vest. 'Look at the state of us,' he said, stroking the ferret's head. 'Me an old crock and you fit to burst on pickled eggs and beer. We'd better change our ways old boy if we want to see Christmas.' He untied Old Sherlock from his belt and thrusting his walking stick into the thin soil, used it as a lever to pull himself up. 'Come on,' he sighed, 'it's time we joined the others. There's life in the old dog yet.'

If only the same could be said of his stick, years of wet weather and woodworm had seen to that. With a loud 'crack' that made Bill look down at his ankles and fear for the worst, the stick snapped in two and sent the poor gentleman first stumbling then rolling down the hillside out of control. What a game for the ferret. Old Sherlock sprinted away down the hill, jumped onboard and for the final 20 yards resembled nothing if not a champion lumberjack spinning his log down the river. But such arrogance was short lived. Bill rolled slap bang into the bottom wall and sent the ferret flying through the air to land in a clump of nettles on the other side.

It was a green and sorry-looking Bill Hicken that looked over the gritstone wall and dribbled. He had over-dosed on dizziness and couldn't remember when he had last felt so ill. A recuperative drink was required, large and alcoholic, only then would his stomach unwind and his brain start spinning in the opposite direction. He edged along the wall to a style and after pulling himself over the top and checking his pockets for change, took one sniff of the evening air and staggered forward like a zombie in the direction of 'The Lamb and Liver Fluke'.

The Reverend Cross prided himself on being a patron of the arts, a regular visitor to Ebenezer Mule's photographic shop in Frogwallop. He would spend many an hour there inspecting the stacks of sepia prints, admiring the Roman slave girls and Greek goddesses but puzzled as to why they should always remind him of the rosy-cheeked lass who served in the chip shop. He would return home of an evening flushed and full of inspiration, and after arranging the furniture in his study would drape his housekeeper in yards of muslin and ask her to look at the birdie. It was a harmless pastime if misunderstood, for who in the village could forget his 'Helen of Troy', a surprising choice for the cover of a parish magazine - not so much the face that launched a thousand ships, as the one that sank the rubber duck. Yet cruel gossip aside, the vicar was the obvious choice to capture Miss Pike's unfortunate condition on film, a photographic record that would seal her removal from the village for good. He had dragged his heavy box camera in front of the crypt, secured the tripod and charged the flash plate, but only with his head under the black velvet drape had he realised his mistake; he had overlooked one essential detail.

'Oh, how bothersome,' he moaned, for while he and the camera were on one side of the crypt door, a very angry Miss Pike was on the other. It was a delicate problem and in the absence of an X-ray tube and a dose of radiation that would exfoliate a mammoth, there was only one option.

'Be a good chap and open the door would you?' He asked one of the villagers only to be faced with stony silence.

'Come now, I have to see the woman to take the picture don't I?'

There was no reply save for the banging and thrashing of Miss Pike as she made her feelings known in the crypt.

'Really, must I do everything?'

He was conscious of the sunlight fading fast outside and the strength of the woman behind the door.

'Please, Miss Pike,' he pleaded. 'Try not to get so upset. I've already said that you're ill, and this banging and thrashing about isn't going to convince me otherwise. The diagnosis is simple, you've been possessed by a demon, a giant rat to be precise, and when the full moon rises you are going to feel most peculiar. All I ask is that you look upon us in a more kindly light and perhaps smile at the camera?'

'Fat chance of that,' commented one of the villagers insisting on keeping the crypt door closed. 'If this 'ere lock fails then we might as well be sprinkled with salt and stand tall like a stick of celery. I say we'd do best to knock her on the head and be done with it.'

'Are you suggesting murder?'

'Not murder, Mr Cross, but sympathy. It'd be like putting down a mad dog.'

'Or a witch,' added another of the group. 'Cos' that's what she is, an evil witch, 'cept no one's had the guts to admit it before. I say we knock her on the head too.'

The vicar was speechless with horror, a condition not shared by the furious Miss Pike who on failing to pull apart the ropes, was trying unsuccessfully to mouth the words of a spell through the handkerchief knotted around her face. It was the '*Stretching of the Cords*,' a simple spell but muffled, and instead of the two ends of the rope sliding slowly apart Arabella heard the snap of knicker elastic and felt a cold wind of change rustle through her gusset. She roared in frustration that only served to harden the villagers' resolve.

'That's torn it; she's on the change. You'll never get your photograph now, Vicar.'

The Reverend Cross considered his options. 'Perhaps, under the circumstances, we should keep the door closed. I could always sketch something for the police. Our statements will suffice as evidence.'

The door to the church swung open, and an excitable Bill Hicken appeared in silhouette against the evening sky. He pointed his finger directly at the vicar and tried to control his anger. 'Idiot, you've let that damned woman escape!'

'What are you talking about, Mr Hicken?'

'That thing, that creature, that Miss Pike – she's taken over the pub! Go and see for yourself if you don't believe me. She's sitting down as bold as brass at the bar, laughing and swearing with the worst of them. It's horrible. What did you fools do, give her a rap on the knuckles and the price of a pint?'

'I have no idea what you mean. Miss Pike is locked away in the crypt. We should know, we bundled her in ourselves.'

'Stuff and nonsense, Vicar. I tell you the creature I saw last night is in

'The Lamb and Liver Fluke' ordering George and Mrs Stubbins about like a couple of skivvies. And she's not alone, there's a whole army of hairy buggers with her drinking the pub dry.'

'Impossible Bill, it can't be true.'

'Are you calling me a liar, old boy? Are you insulting the regiment?'

'I'm doing no such thing. All I'm saying is that Miss Pike is over there behind the crypt door. I'd stake my life on it.'

'Then why don't you open the door and see if she's still there, no harm in that, surely?'

'Are you a complete idiot? There's every harm – if Miss Pike is in the pub then we have all made a mistake, but if she's not....well, I need hardly spell out the consequences.' But apparently he did, for in the time it took the vicar to dismiss Bill's outburst as the wild ramblings of a drunk, Miss Pike had succeeded in untying and spitting out her gag. Her addiction to boiled sweets had helped. She had twisted the gag around to the front and by virtue of an upper molar roll, a half-nelson twist and a tuneless whistle had pulled the knot apart. The rope was a different matter. In the absence of any sharp edges only magic would suffice, and there was only so much knicker elastic to snap if she fumbled the words again. Arabella concentrated hard and closed her eyes. There was a fizzle and a smell of burning before the rope fell to the floor behind her. She snarled in anger; a Prometheus unchained with a revolver and a handbag full of explosive.

Bill Hicken was arguing with the vicar. 'Go and see for yourself. I tell you, it's Miss Pike in that pub. Dammit, man, we're wasting time. We should form a barricade across the street and arm ourselves to the teeth. What do you say?'

'Don't rush me, Bill. You have me confused.'

A pistol fired, and the lock to the crypt shattered. Before the vicar realised what had happened, Arabella kicked the door open and stared at her captors.

'All of you stay where you are!' she shouted. 'There are five bullets in this pistol and a pocketful in my coat. I've been jumped on, gagged, trussed up like an old ham and locked in a crypt. Give me one good reason I shouldn't pull this trigger.'

'Miss Pike!' the vicar interrupted, his hands clasped together in mock gratitude. 'You're still a woman and the moon now full in the sky. What a pleasant surprise, and such a terrible misunderstanding too.'

Miss Pike made no effort to reply but indicated with a sweep of her pistol that the vicar should continue with his explanation.

'How silly, we seem to have mistaken you for a horrid beast that has recently invaded our village...' The vicar paused mid-sentence; this was not what he had intended to say at all.

'Mistook me for something *horrid*, did you say?'

'Absolutely, Miss Pike,' he whispered. 'Although to tell you the truth only the Stubbinses and Bill Hicken have set eyes on the creature. Such a lurid description – horrid, hairy, and frightening – I can't say I discern the resemblance myself, you being so charming and statuesque, quite the *'Venus de Milo'* in fact.'

'What are you trying to say, Vicar? That none of this was personal, merely unfortunate, that you were an unwilling subordinate in the day's proceedings?'

'Exactly Miss Pike, you have it in one.'

'Then you are a liar and a fool,' sneered Arabella and pushed the vicar away. 'You there,' she said looking at Bill Hicken. 'You seem an honest fellow, tell me about this creature and don't spare the details; I'm not as thin-skinned as the Vicar seems to believe.'

'Wait on, Ma'am. Things are happening a little too fast here. Five minutes ago you were a rat in a pub. Now you're back to your old self, standing in front of me with not a sign of fur and whiskers. I don't know about the Vicar, but I'm confused.'

Arabella stared at each villager in turn. 'Listen to me carefully,' she said, 'and that goes for all of you. I am not and never have been a rodent. I have never heard of anything so ridiculous. If you continue with this moor-peep fantasy then I shall turn into something far worse, far more frightening and far more deadly. Do I make myself clear?' She pulled the hammer back on the pistol. There was much nodding of heads and mutterings of agreement. 'Good, I'm glad we understand each other. So, Mr Hicken, tell me what you saw.'

Bill gave an accurate and worrying account of what he had seen through the smoke stained windows of 'The Lamb and Liver Fluke;' Vermyn Stench, the army of giant rats and poor George and his wife running around the tap room like a pair of headless chickens. It was what Arabella and the professor had feared.

'How many of these creatures do you think we're dealing with?' Arabella asked.

'About twenty, if all of them are in the pub that is.'

'Oh dear, that many? Well, Mr Hicken, you were once in the army. What's your assessment of the situation? Do you think we can overpower them?'

'Why should we want to do that?' interrupted the Reverend Cross, still feeling hurt from being called a liar and a fool. 'We're far safer here inside the church. We should wait until they've gone.'

'But they are here for a purpose. It's me they want.'

'It seems to me,' the vicar said addressing his comments to the villagers, 'that Miss Pike knows a lot more about the situation than she is letting on. I suggest some explanation is required before we do anything else.'

Arabella sighed. 'I could try to explain, but I fear no one will believe me, particularly you Vicar. The situation is far too complicated, but what I *can* say is that the life of a young prince depends upon my freedom and your cooperation. You must not allow me to be captured.'

'Too complicated to understand, poppycock!' sneered the vicar. 'Who do you think we are, children? You insult us, Miss Pike, with your amateur dramatics. I ask you this – who are those creatures? Where do they come from?'

It was no good; Arabella was going to have to say something, even if it was the smallest of white lies. 'They are spies from a foreign country. They have orders to smuggle me away to...' She was tempted to say France. It would have made little difference. During the Napoleonic wars, an unfortunate monkey washed up on an English shore was tried and hung as a French spy. 'Oh, very well, you may as well know. They come from Berumbia.'

'Berumbia?' Almost to a person the villagers repeated the name, for although it was absolute dribble and the only word Arabella could think of on the spur of the moment, it sounded suitably foreign, exotic even. Perhaps it was an island in the South Seas full of barbarous tribes and portly women dressed up in too little silk for mystery or comfort. With this single word Arabella's character was transformed. She was no witch at all but a romantic heroine, nothing short of a Scheherazade. How dare those filthy spies attempt to drag her back to the Sultan's tent, and as for the Reverend Cross? Well, he should be ashamed, for where was his so-called charity now? No, in that fleeting moment Arabella could do no wrong.

'Don't worry, Miss Pike,' assured Bill Hicken speaking for most of the villagers present. 'We won't let those natives lay a claw on you. It won't be easy, mind; I saw all manner of weapons through the window. I'd say the most we could come up with would be a few shotguns and your pistol.'

'Then I shall send for help. I have friends who are out shooting on Grimspittle Moor. They could be with us soon.'

'Oh yes?' asked the Vicar sarcastically. 'And how are they going to get here, fly?'

Arabella ignored the comment and took a pen and a piece of paper from her pocket. She scribbled some words then disappeared outside. The sound of a large hen being chased and pounced upon was heard, and then to the amazement of all, the clucking and squawking stopped only to be replaced by a loud 'whoosh' like a bonfire rocket being set off in the street. In the absence of a homing pigeon, this poultry telegram was the best Arabella could come up with.

'They say that given enough time and a typewriter a bunch of monkeys could write Shakespeare, but throw them a map and tell them to fold it away and they'd be buggered!' These were some of the sarcastic comments that the Sisterhood were laughing and giggling over as for the umpteenth time that evening a gust of wind blew Professor Arbutus Broadbent and his maps all over the heather.

'A little help wouldn't go amiss,' he shouted picking himself up and dusting himself off, for much to his annoyance Bethesda Chubb and her colleagues were sheltering behind a gritstone wall and leaving himself to do all the work. The ladies ignored his temper and continued with their conversation, uncharitable snippets of which could be heard on the wind.

'…perhaps, on a dark night with a lamp post behind him, but not with those eyebrows, they'd have to go…'

'…and those ears, I've a cardigan back home with less hairs…'

The professor was equally scathing. 'Ridiculous women,' he muttered. 'Worst thing the Sisterhood did was to recruit the Southern Chapter – and as for that Miss Chubb, she's nothing but trouble; too young, too wild and too damn fond of herself.'

The professor was not in the best of moods. He had escorted Bethesda Chubb and her companions to Grimspittle Moor and they had done nothing but complain about the mud, the weather and the weight of the wooden crate they had been ordered to carry. Years of good living had made them soft. The first thing he would do on his return to Grubdale would be to organise some exercise. A few weekends spent dangling from viaducts, scampering up cliffs and wading through ice-cold streams should see them right. 'Ladies, please!' he implored. 'Help me search this ground; the pegs must be here somewhere.'

'OK, keep your hair on, I'm coming,' said Bethesda Chubb. She stood to her feet, stretched her arms and cried out in dismay as a gust of wind blew the policeman's helmet off her head and high up in the evening sky. 'Now see what's happened. I'm going to have to pick a quarrel with another constable. If you only knew the trouble it takes to find a helmet that fits.'

'The less I know about your Suffragette evenings, the better, Miss Chubb. This façade of politics will get us in trouble, mark my words. I sometimes think you and your Chapter believe in the rubbish that Pankhurst woman spouts. You should follow Miss Pike's example. She keeps herself to herself and is loved by the community, by everyone Miss Chubb, not just the ladies. Now look to your feet and get the others to help. There are four pegs to find.'

It had been years since the professor and the Sisterhood had escaped from Vivarium. They had followed the glowing tunnel of a wyrmhole through space to where they now stood, shivering and wet with mist on Grimspittle Moor. They had marked the area by hammering steel pegs into the ground, and although it had seemed a good idea at the time, now, after hours of searching on all fours in the cold wind and drizzle, perhaps a large neon sign flashing the words 'Not Here You Idiot, There!' would have been a better choice.

The professor stubbed his toe, tripped over his feet and, to the ladies' astonishment, his head and shoulders disappeared into thin air.

'And about time too,' laughed Bethesda standing tall in the heather with her hands on her hips. 'At least he's good for something. Come on you lot, gather round, I think the Professor's found what we were looking for.'

The professor re-appeared hopping on one foot and with his hair sticking out in all directions. 'Damned static electricity,' he cursed trying to smooth it down.

'Well done, Prof!' said Bethesda landing him a hearty slap between the shoulder blades and laughed to see the poor man stumble forward once more into the portal. He crawled back with his hair like Medusa after sticking her tongue in an electrical socket.

'So what now?' asked one of the ladies tired of standing around in the cold.

'What now? Don't you see? The Professor's stumbled upon the wyrmhole!'

'Yes, thank you Miss Chubb, I'll take it from here.' Professor Broadbent raised himself to his feet and shook the sparks from his head. 'Right, we should check for footprints; that's the next thing we must do. If this is where Stench and his rats appeared, then there are sure to be signs of entry.'

'But I can only see our footprints, no one else's.'

'Nonsense, what do you mean, *our* footprints?'

Alas, in the confusion of the search, what with the professor and the Sisterhood trampling through the heather and wet soil, any sign of the enemy's footprints had been long since destroyed.

'Oh no,' moaned the professor. 'This is impossible. We're no better off than we started. Stench could have come from anywhere.'

'But he didn't, did he. See what I've found here.' Bethesda handed over a small dagger with a twisted transparent blade. 'I'm no expert, but I hardly think it's Sheffield steel.'

Professor Broadbent removed his spectacles and examined the knife's handle more closely. 'Excellent work, Miss Chubb, a timely discovery if ever there was one. Look at these carvings and the peculiar metal of the blade. I'd say for certain that it came from the Sorcerer's workshop, wouldn't you?'

Bethesda nodded in agreement.

'Good, then that's settled. We shall remain here on guard. If Stench or his re-enforcements appear then, we'll blast them to kingdom come. Well, ladies, you each have a sleeping bag in your rucksack. I'll leave the domestic arrangements to you, but a cup of tea would be nice. In the meantime, Miss Chubb, if you wouldn't mind opening our crate. We might as well hand out the weapons, seeing as we're supposed to be a shooting party.'

Professor Broadbent strode across to the wall and, feeling pleased with himself, sat down out of the wind. 'Don't forget to fill the lining of your sleeping bags with heather,' he suggested. 'It will help keep you warm and comfortable.'

The ladies looked at each other, puzzled. Was the professor expecting them to sleep out here on the moor? Surely not, for didn't the words 'shooting party' and 'shooting lodge' go together, with perhaps 'hot tub' and 'slap-up meal' appearing on the same page? Some the group made a great show of screwing their faces up in disgust and flicking sheep-droppings away with their fingers. Bethesda, more keen than was felt necessary by the others, walked over to the crate and prized open the lid. Her face lit up as she surveyed the various delights within, for amongst the shotguns and cartridges lay the marvel of a machine gun and tripod. 'Bags I for guard duty!' she shouted, lifting the heavy weapon out and placing it on the ground. The professor nodded agreement and indicated with his hand where she should place the machine gun for maximum cover; an old tumbledown hide that overlooked the entrance to the wyrmhole. A few of the ladies shook their heads and after arming themselves with shotguns from the crate, accompanied Bethesda to the small, three-sided building.

'What about a few practise shots?' the professor called out and began to wind up a clockwork seagull he had unfolded from his coat pocket. 'First one to blow it to pieces gets a bar of chocolate.' He threw the mechanical bird in the air then sat back to watch the entertainment as one by one the ladies cracked open their shotguns and loaded them with ammunition. It was almost dark now and the target was difficult to see, but as it flapped and soared past the hide a cannonade of gunfire sent out a deadly hail of pellets to the front and a line of startled and winded ladies sliding backwards to the rear.

'Don't forget, hold the stock tight against the shoulder,' the professor advised. 'Otherwise the recoil can give you a nasty kick.'

The seagull flew upwards in a loop and approached the front of the hide for a second time. Again the volley of gunshots slammed forth and again the unfortunate ladies slid back.

'Missed!' called out the professor.

'Up yours!' shouted someone else. And so the game continued with the tiny clockwork motor never seeming to run down. The bird swooped and soared as though it was being controlled by the professor, while the ladies, forsaking the hide, ran and tripped and ran after their target again.

'Be careful where you aim!' warned the professor as the seagull dived low and two lines of surprised ladies found themselves looking down the barrels of each other's guns. Such near misses aside, the chase was proving fun and good practice too. By the time the evening light had failed and the white paint of the seagull could no longer be seen, everyone save Bethesda was a reasonable shot. Poor Bethesda, no matter how hard she had dragged the barrel of the machine gun around, she still couldn't raise it high enough to point at the target. She had cursed and sweated for a quarter of an hour before giving up in a huff and was now in a trigger-happy mood best left where she was until her temper improved. And then along came the hen.

What an unfortunate bird the hen was. It had been out pecking of an evening when some mountain of a human had grabbed it from behind, an occasion usually proceeded by what was known in the hen coop as the 'one-way stretch.' But the inevitable failed, there was no pulling of the neck, no 'snap' and then darkness, and no waking up as a juicy grub in the mountains of Tibet. Instead, a roll of paper had been tied to its foot, sparkling glitter sprinkled over its back and then a glorious warm feeling followed by an uncontrollable urge to flap and fly for England. Somewhere in its small brain the bird knew this to be wrong. Why this sudden rush of air and the sight of rooftops disappearing below? The hen looked down between its legs and seemed to accept the fact that a large jet of flame was shooting out of its nether regions and propelling it at great speed up and away over the countryside with nothing more than a slight itch to be felt from behind. It clucked with pleasure as it rolled, looped and snaked through the sky, unaware that with each flick of its wings the bird was being drawn irresistibly in the direction of Grimspittle Moor. Such a pity that whatever blend of magic was providing the propulsion, it was as a microwave oven to the most intimate parts of the hen's anatomy. The first of the eggs exploded over Frogwallop causing pain, surprise and a report of a comet in the Derbyshire Times. The remainder of the clutch succeeded in sending the hapless creature spinning in flames on its way down to earth.

'Incoming!' shouted one of the Sisterhood as she saw the trail of fire and sparks in the sky. But as luck would have it, the hen managed to regain some of its control before making an emergency landing, skidding and bouncing along the heather. It clucked in distress on catching a glimpse of its parson's nose before exploding into a cloud of pillow stuffing as Bethesda squeezed the trigger of the machine gun.

'Supper's up!' she laughed.

'Poor blighter,' mumbled Professor Broadbent, turning the smouldering remains over with his foot. 'There's not enough left for soup let alone supper – wait a minute, what's this?' He crouched down and after striking a match and holding the flame in his cupped hands, retrieved the charred message from what remained of a drumstick.

'Don't overdo it,' Bethesda called out as the professor whooped and danced in a circle. 'I mean, it wasn't as though I could miss at that range, the stupid bird landed in front of me.'

'Never mind about that,' he said as he ran back to the hide. 'There's been a change of plans. Gather round all of you, come on chop-chop!'

'What's up now?' asked a sleepy voice from beneath a blanket. 'Has Bethesda shot the professor in his foot?'

'Asleep are we? I thought you were on guard? No, for once I have good news. Magic up a fire someone; it's too dark to see anything by.'

Bethesda clapped her hands and a small tussock of heather burst into flames.

'Excellent, if a little close for comfort. Now then ladies, I have a note here from Arabella. The news is what we've hoped for – the enemy has made its first mistake. Unfurl the flag of Wyrm and charge your guns, for tonight we steal a march on Sodden. Stench has arrived with barely twenty troops to call his own. These are favourable odds, and we have the element of surprise. *Carpe diem* – seize the moment my dear friends, seize the day!'

'*Carpe farte* if you ask me,' murmured the voice from beneath the blanket. 'Seize the old windbag and let me get some sleep.

Professor Broadbent continued with his speech. 'Don't look so scared, there's nothing to be frightened of but defeat itself. We shall fly to Sodden under cover of darkness and swoop down on our enemy like a hawk. Be cruel and merciless, but be wary. We must never underestimate what Stench can do. He has the power of dissipation so don't waste your time with spells. Are we understood?'

The ladies looked at each other then slowly nodded their heads.

'Good, then hold out your pockets so Miss Chubb can distribute what's left of the cartridges. By the way, Miss Chubb, I need you to guard the wyrmhole while we're gone.'

'You mean I can't join in the fight?'

'Not exactly, you see I need someone brave and dependable to protect our rear. I can think of no other person than your good self.'

'Really?'

'Yes, Miss Chubb. Now choose a friend for company. The two of you and the machine gun should be sufficient, but just to be certain I'll leave you some 'jam' as well – one pot do you think?'

Bethesda nodded eagerly and accepted her reward; a pot of the professor's finest explosive.

'Excellent, I knew I could count on you. We'll be back as soon as the fighting is over. Just make sure not to shoot us down that's all.'

Professor Broadbent rummaged about in the bottom of the crate as the ammunition was handed out and lifted the last of its contents on the ground, a small foldaway chair with a golf bag attached. He took great care to position it away from the flames of the fire and sat down on the canvas seat. 'Don't worry, I'm coming with you,' he said pulling on a pair of goggles over his eyes. 'Are we ready? Good, then let's be off.' He tugged at a ripcord on the side of the golf bag and a large balloon in the shape of a fish inflated with a 'bang' and rose up in the air over his head. 'Rather clever, don't you think?' he said peering out from what appeared to be a cage of strings attaching the balloon to the chair. But the ladies merely stood there, silent and astonished as, like the unfortunate hen before him, the professor was pulled up into the night sky at an alarming rate.

'Of course, it's not perfect,' he shouted. 'I may need a tow.' So one by one his companions made the sign of the cross and with a puff of purple smoke appearing at their feet, floated up towards the professor. They took hold of a string apiece and turned the balloon around in the direction of Frogwallop. 'Well, what are we waiting for?' he asked, bobbing up and down and feeling slightly unwell. 'Onwards to glory and don't spare the horses!' and with the battle cry still wet on his lips, Professor Broadbent found himself accelerating at great speed as he was dragged forward.

Chapter Six

ENTER THE DRAGON

Any stranger to Sodden would be forgiven for believing it the most peculiar of rural villages, if not the very capital of moor-peep-dom. Its only pub, 'The 'Lamb and Liver Fluke,' was full to the brim with giant hairy beasts, swigging back tankards of cloudy ale and shooting pistols into the ceiling, whilst outside in the street a hastily formed village militia was attempting to be as quiet as possible as they carried pews from the local church and laid them across the road in the form of a barricade, a task made all the more difficult by the protests of the Reverend Ainsley Cross, who sat stubbornly on each pew as they were borne out aloft.

'I don't care if *all* of you promised to help Miss Pike,' he moaned as he was transported yet again from the church. 'These are holy fittings and fixtures!'

'Oh stop nagging Vicar; they're nothing but old oak benches and full of woodworm at that. Think of it as charity and lend a hand.'

'I shall do no such thing; the great Miss Pike can fight her battles without me. She considers my skills second to Mr Hicken.'

This was the source of his petulance. Arabella had chosen Bill Hicken as her deputy and made no secret of thinking the vicar a fool. As for Mr Hicken, he was as proud as any old soldier lost in retirement could have been. He had hurried home to collect his medals and regimental sword and now stood breathless in ragged splendour, every inch the military hero.

And what would the stranger have made of the villagers now crouched behind the pews and armed with what few weapons they could find? Were they not foolish in their eagerness to please? In truth, they were ashamed. In their moment of need with 'The Lamb and Liver Fluke' overrun and George Stubbins and his wife held hostage, it was Miss Pike who had remained calm and taken control of the situation. The very woman they had kidnapped and bundled into the church cellar was now a paragon of forgiveness and fortitude. It made them feel all the more wretched. Of course, the money had helped, and such a lot of money too, for it seemed that Arabella's leather holdall was a bottomless pit of gold sovereigns. 'Bribery and corruption', the vicar had muttered before looking inside the open bag and smiling.

Bill Hicken tapped Arabella on the shoulder and pointed to the front of the pub where a sudden flood of light from an opening door revealed the outline of a huddled figure holding a suitcase.

'Looks as though we might have a bit of action after all Ma'am,' he said and Arabella nodded in agreement. She cocked the hammer of her revolver and aimed the short stub of the barrel at whoever stood in front.

'Gentlemen, your weapons if you please,' whispered Bill Hicken. There was a general rattling of metal on wood as a crude collection of firearms and catapults appeared over the top of the barricade. The noise startled the figure in the doorway. It stepped out into the street and from the light of the open door, was revealed in all its fur; a horrid mountain of a rat in clumsy boots and with two large cream ears like saucers on top of its head.

'Take aim gentlemen,' continued Bill Hicken, his memory floating back to a small besieged outpost on the plains of Africa. But before he could shout 'FIRE', the door of the pub slammed shut and sent the giant rat running and stumbling forward towards the barricade.

'Bugger this for a game of soldiers, I'm off,' hissed a rather cowardly member of the village militia, dropping his garden fork and turning to flee. But before he could be grabbed by the collar and dragged back into line, a fur coat fell off the shoulders of the charging 'rat' to reveal poor Mrs Stubbins in a knitted grey balaclava with one of her brassieres pinned on top. She ran past the amazed onlookers and made off in the direction of her mother's house, blissfully unaware of the fright she had caused or the sudden death she had narrowly escaped.

The villagers, somewhat unsettled, returned their concentration to the street where Mrs Stubbins' best fur coat now lay in the dirt, a string of sausages pinned to its back to complete the disguise.

'Urgh,' shivered a young man with a bruise on his chin, crouching next to Arabella, 'that was a horrid sight'.

'Don't fret lad, you've seen far worse,' reassured a friend, which sparked off a small discussion from the group. For while the image of Mrs Stubbins running and screaming like a banshee was indeed frightening, it was considered nothing compared to 'Venus at her Toilet', another photograph by the vicar that had adorned the cover of the parish magazine the year before.

'Aye, you're right there Jack,' quipped one of the villagers, 'Just keep thinking about that housekeeper up at the Vicarage and nowt'll scare you.'

The vicar ignored the laughter and tried to change the subject. 'A clever plan dressing up as a rat don't you think?' he said from the safety of the church gate. 'Rather better than this 'Siege of Delhi'. No doubt Mr Stubbins will come up with something equally ingenious.'

The villagers didn't have long to wait. As if on cue the front window of 'The Lamb and Liver Fluke' exploded into a shower of glass as something large and undignified, with a colander strapped to its head, flew through the air and bounced painfully on the ground.

'At my command, AIM!' shouted Bill Hicken holding his regimental sword aloft, and once again a collection of firearms appeared over the top of the barricade.

'Well I never,' said the vicar. 'Being thrown from a building to affect an escape; highly original. I'd lower your weapons if I were you unless you want to shoot poor Mr Stubbins by mistake.'

The hapless George rose unsteadily to his feet and, seeing friendly faces in the distance, wobbled and stumbled in the general direction of the barricade. But unfortunately for the landlord, whoever had thrown him across the full length of the bar was now unwilling for such a delightful game to end. Two soldier rats leapt through the broken window and grabbed George by the back of his collar. They steered their victim around and marched him off towards the front door, indicating with ever wider sweeps of their arms bigger and better flight paths to come. George looked back sadly in the direction of his friends, his bottom lip quivering.

'FIRE!' shouted Bill Hicken slicing his sword through the air, but despite such a dramatic gesture no gunfire was heard. The two soldier rats let go of George's arm and turned around with flintlocks drawn, aware for the first time of a barricade in the darkly-lit street and a collection of firearms, now shaking uncontrollably, appearing over the top. Bill Hicken looked quickly to his right and left to check what had happened to the expected volley, and returned his concentration to the two rats in front.

'Those of you with your fingers on the trigger,' said Bill with some urgency, 'perhaps now would be a good time to squeeze.' There was the roar of three shotguns being fired followed by the sharp 'crack' of Arabella's pistol. The colander on George's head jumped up in the air and span around in a half circle, while the brickwork above the pub door was peppered with shot. Only a lucky hit with a catapult caused one of the rats to fall backwards and spit out a few of its teeth.

'Too high, try again!' shouted Bill Hicken. But the second volley was no better and this time both of the rats managed to fire their flintlocks off in the general direction of Arabella but to no effect.

'What's the matter with you all?' asked the vicar crawling towards the barricade. 'We made mince meat of those rats yesterday.'

'Aye, they were only little buggers but just look at 'em now. I tell you I'm scared. No one told me they could shoot back!'

'Here, give that shotgun to me before they grab hold of poor Mr Stubbins for a second time.' The vicar managed to wrestle the gun off the villager and aim it in front.

'Come on George!' he shouted. 'Run to us while you have a chance!' George turned around from the door of the pub and still on shaking legs made an erratic approach towards the barricade.

'That's it George!' called out the other villagers in encouragement. 'Don't look behind you, just keep running. No, this way George, this way!'

Arabella joined in, urging the landlord forward as the two soldier rats loaded their antique firearms and made ready to aim. She leant over the top of the barricade and stretched out her arm in assistance, waiting to grab George by the hand and pull him up over the stacked pews. George took one look at her and stopped in his tracks.

'It's alright Mr Stubbins,' she urged. 'It's me, Miss Pike. Hurry up and grab my hand, I won't bite.' This was a poor choice of words. George stared at Arabella for a few moments then turned to face the pub, not sure of what to do next. A crack of pistol fire and the whistle of two bullets passing by his head decided the matter; he fell to the ground and whimpered like a child

'How dare they shoot at me!' protested the vicar and immediately let fire with both barrels, destroying the heads of the two soldier rats in a fountain of gore. He dropped the shotgun and covered his mouth with his hand. 'Oh dear,' he said, his face turning white with nausea, 'Did I do that?'

'Good shooting Mr Cross!' shouted Bill Hicken. 'Keep that up old boy and the fight will soon be over.'

'Do you think so? It's just that I never realised there'd be so much blood.'

This was the consensus of the 'militia' as well, who to a man were beginning to get cold feet and upset stomachs about the whole escapade. Shooting small rats was one thing but these creatures were nearly as tall as a human and pumped up to breaking point with blood and giblets. It was enough to put a man off his black pudding let alone his tomato soup.

Arabella noticed a sudden stillness in the air. The shooting and shouting from within 'The Lamb and Liver Fluke' had stopped, and now a mob of soldier rats had gathered behind the broken window and were looking out onto the street.

'Will someone pick up that gun and load it,' she asked. 'We're going to need every firearm we can use.'

The Reverend Cross obeyed, keeping one eye on the soldier rats in front but then handed the shotgun back to the empty-handed villager.

'You'd better keep this,' he said 'I don't think it's appropriate in my hands.'

Arabella threw him her holdall.

'If you want to help then stay back there and look after the money; if the worst comes to the worst then at least the church will have a new roof.'

'Very droll I don't think,' he answered.

The body of rats in the window were pushed roughly aside, and the figure of Vermyn Stench appeared amongst them.

'I take it the ugly one's the boss?' asked the vicar and Arabella nodded seeing her adversary in the flesh for the first time.

'Then God help us.'

Vermyn Stench removed the remaining few shards of glass from the window with wild sweeps of his cane then climbed through the large opening to look directly at Arabella. He sniffed the air with one long intake of breath then shaking his head with distaste, spat out a trail of spittle from his mouth.

'Apparently I don't smell nice, Mr Hicken. I assume that's what he's telling me. Well, two can play at that game.' Arabella inhaled in an equally dramatic fashion then waving her hand in front of her nose pretended to faint. Vermyn Stench glared with rage and resisted the impulse to check his armpits. He bent over double with his bottom pointing in the direction of Arabella, and began to stamp his feet and wave his tail from side to side in time to an imaginary rhythm. Just as Arabella was thinking this too good a target to miss, he jumped around to face her again and proceeded to shake his stomach and flick his tongue in and out, all the time stamping his feet as before.

'Amazing coordination the creature shows, Mr Hicken. Do we have any idea what the dance means?'

'Perhaps best if we didn't translate, Ma'am. The last time I saw something similar was back in New Zealand, just before the Maori charged. Look, see, the whole lot of 'em's at it.'

Arabella looked on in amazement as the remainder of the soldier rats climbed out into the street and copied the peculiar movement and facial gymnastics of their leader.

'You mean to say that they're trying to scare us?'

'Aye Ma'am and no doubt with a lot of insults thrown in as well.'

'Really, then let's give them a taste of their own medicine. In for a penny in for a pound, isn't that what you say up here in the North?'

Arabella took off her tweed jacket, rolled up the sleeves of her lambs' wool jumper and, to the horror of everyone behind the barricade, proceeded to bump, grind, wobble and swear like a trooper.

'You…..you spawn of Satan!' exclaimed the vicar, not knowing whether to cover his eyes, put his fingers in his ears, or else rush back to the church and get his camera. Arabella ignored him and retrieved her jacket.

'Round one to us don't you think?' she said, and Bill Hicken nodded in agreement.

'Well done ma'am, you've got his attention.'

Vermyn Stench had stopped moving and was staring agape at this primeval force of a woman. A final gesture was required; the etiquette of war demanded it of him, if not his pride. He trawled the depths and made the universal sign for stuffing the turkey, an action that was at once taken up and repeated by the soldier rats now standing behind him.

'Well I never!' exclaimed Arabella, 'I don't think we need a dictionary to translate that sordid little mime. No artistry, no finesse at all. Mr Hicken, please inform the others I'll give ten guineas to the next man who can shoot the filth out of that rancid creature's brain.'

'Ten sovereigns you say, Ma'am? I could do with some of that. Here, give us your revolver.' Bill Hicken took careful aim and emptied the remainder of the chamber in the direction of Vermyn's head. He lowered the gun, but Vermyn Stench remained as he stood, sneering in contempt at his attacker.

'Impossible, I could have sworn I was on target!'

'You were,' whispered Arabella, look...', for Stench was now hitting the side of his face and making a great show of spitting out the four flattened bullets one by one.

'Well, I've never seen anything like that before. I hope you can run Ma'am,' Bill said. 'Cos we ain't gonna hold out behind this barricade for long.' He pointed to Vermyn Stench with the empty revolver. 'Not with the Great Houdini over there.'

There was no reply from Miss Pike. Bill looked around and saw her standing on one foot like a pitcher in a game of baseball. She spun her arm around three times then threw something at the figure of the snarling man rat, a small party balloon that shot away from her hand and flew hither and thither as the air escaped.

'What on earth is that woman doing?' asked the vicar. Arabella shook her head, wiped her brow, and then tried again. This time a stream of wet spaghetti flew out from her jacket cuffs and fell with a 'schlopp' at Stench's feet. He turned the pile of pasta over with his toes then looked back at this strange woman; a pathetic figure who was hitting the air with her fists and cursing her incompetence. Was this the best the Sisterhood had to offer? Stench didn't wait to find out but swung his cane suddenly around in a wide circle. There was a flash of lightning and a thunderclap, and two of the militia found themselves hurled backwards into the upper branches of a sycamore tree. Before the unfortunate pair could slide slowly to the ground and roll about in agony, Vermyn Stench swung his cane around for a second time and roared at the top of his voice. This time there was no magic. Stench had given the signal to charge. The rat soldiers leapt forward as one, running helter-skelter towards the barricade, abandoning their crude firearms for the wicked curved daggers and scimitars held around their waists.

Bill Hicken had been expecting the move. 'Pick your targets well gentlemen,' he shouted. 'Let every shot count.' He waited until the rats were a few yards away then gave the order to fire, but the remainder of the village militia were now running back down the street to the safety of their respective homes. He lifted his sword ready for the onslaught and prepared himself for a soldier's death while Arabella fumbled about with her pockets trying to find the bullets to reload her revolver. George Stubbins pulled himself to his feet and stood up between them, still dazed but now armed with a rusty gun that had been left behind by one of the villagers; a peculiar museum piece shaped like a trumpet. He took one look at the rampaging horde scrambling over the barricade and closed his eyes. There was a tremendous roar of gunshot, and the leading rats disintegrated into a myriad of sticky pieces, covering everything around in a thick coating of giblets and fur. Those rats that followed stopped still in their tracks then hurried back in panic and retrieved their firearms. Who cared if their boss was indestructible; *they* were decidedly fragile young things where buckshot was concerned.

Behind the barricade, three crimson-drenched figures each spat out a gobbet of rat's blood and wiped the covering of gore from their eyes, amazed at finding themselves still alive and the soldier rats retreating. George looked down at his peculiar firing piece in wonder while Arabella and Bill Hicken patted him on the back and called him a fine fellow, all the time taking care to point the weapon away from each other and back towards the pub. But George was innocent. He pulled the trigger accidentally and following a small retort and release of smoke, a few hobnails and floor tacks fell out on the floor. The three exchanged looks of puzzlement then dived for cover as another roar of gunshot caused the ground around Vermyn Stench's feet to explode into dust.

'Hello down there!' shouted Professor Broadbent from the comfort of his balloon chair. I hope we're not too late?'

Arabella looked upwards. Some of the Sisterhood were hovering overhead, reloading their shotguns. The professor, pulling on one of the cords that attached his foldaway chair to the balloon, began rather too quick a descent to the barricade below. He jumped from the chair before it crashed into the side of the church pews, and landed less skilfully than originally planned next to Arabella.

'We came as quickly as we could,' he said leaning on her shoulder and rubbing his ankle, 'and I see from your appearance, not a minute too soon. I take it all this blood is not yours, Miss Pike? Of course not, a silly question to ask.' He tested the weight of his body on his foot then stood up straight.

'So this is the terrible Vermyn Stench,' he continued, limping around her in a circle. 'Well, what are you waiting for Miss Pike, shoot him down.'

Arabella restrained herself from pushing the professor over the top of the barricade with a single swipe of her arm. She merely stared at him in anger then in calm, precise detail spelt out the obvious.

'So, Stench is impervious to bullets as well as magic is he?' said the professor, stroking his chin and examining this deadly adversary who was now staring up into the night sky and trying to make out where the gunfire had come from.

'Fascinating; but hardly the best news I've heard today. There must be some reason, some talisman he is wearing perhaps?'

'You don't say?' said Arabella with more than a hint of sarcasm in her voice. She was blotting what she could of the soldier rats from her jacket with her best linen handkerchief and was not particularly impressed.

Another volley of gunfire broke the silence as Stench was thrown backwards with the sheer force of lead shot hitting him in the chest. His coat was now a mass of tattered blue gabardine and frayed silver facings, and in his fury Stench tore the garment from his shoulders and threw it at his feet.

'Is that your band uniform George?' joked Bill Hicken attempting to find his own medals amongst the mess of blood and guts splattered on his chest. The landlord nodded forlornly.

'Pity that, it looks ruined now.'

Vermyn Stench was furious. He could see the small group of figures hovering and swooping through the air above him, each taking turns to fire off two barrels.

'Don't waste your ammunition ladies, you can't hurt him!' pleaded the professor, but it was too late. A panic had broken out above the barricade and soon all but a handful of cartridge shells remained. Vermyn pushed himself upright from the pub wall and covered his face with his steel hook, for although the Sorcerer had made him indestructible, each round of shot stung like fire as it struck home. He pointed his cane towards the middle of the flying women and sketched a figure of eight rapidly in the air. The silver claw at its tip opened out, and then with a flash of sparks snapped suddenly shut sending each of the Sisterhood plummeting to the ground. Some were lucky and bounced through the branches of overhanging trees, while a few hit the ground hard and rolled around where they lay, crying out in agony and rubbing their wounds.

'That device will be the death of us,' said Professor Broadbent staring intently at the silver claw on the tip of Stench's cane. 'Some wand of dispelling I shouldn't wonder. As long as he has it in his grasp then our chance of using magic is lost. If we're to make progress tonight, then we must destroy it or take it from him. Here, give me your sword.'

The professor snatched the regimental sword from Bill Hicken and tested the suppleness and edge of the blade against the wooden pews.

'This will have to do, although I shall need all my strength to cleave that cane from his grasp.

'Well Miss Pike, wish me luck and let us hope this Stench is an arrogant brute. I intend to challenge him to a duel. If the creature makes a meal of me, then your only choice is to blow him and the street up with that jar of explosive I gave you in the holdall.'

There was a frantic coughing and spluttering from behind as the Reverend Cross quickly replaced the lid on a small pot and attempted not to swallow. He was having a minor crisis of faith after seeing a small group of angels in the night sky all looking like Miss Pike and had taken a spoonful of 'jam' for comfort. Now he was a walking time bomb with a mouthful of fire and a holdall of explosive in his lap. He stared forlornly at Miss Pike, whimpering and pointing to his mouth, his jacket and his trousers smoking from the scattering of tiny holes burnt through by his dribble. Arabella ran as fast as she could to the vicar pleading with him not to spit. She pulled him to his feet and dragged him back into the church, all the time keeping her hand over his mouth.

'Just do what I tell you, Vicar, it's your only chance. You've explosive enough in your mouth to blow a large hole in the floor.'

It was difficult to make out what the vicar mumbled in reply, but just to be on the safe side Arabella crossed herself and curtsied at the altar. She pushed him forward up the numerous steps to the top of the belfry, then leaning the vicar against the inner wall asked him to spit as far and as carefully as he could through the small stone grill leading outside.

'This way you get to keep your legs,' she explained crouching down behind one of the church bells and putting her fingers in her ears. The vicar needed no encouragement; he was breathless from the climb and fighting every instinct to swallow. He let fly with a gobbet of spit that would have put a camel to shame. There followed a few seconds of silence in which the poor man fell back behind the great church bell, and then a large explosion occurred that sent showers of dust descending over the two crouched figures and caused a large crack to appear all the way up the church steeple. There was some other noise too; a deep groan that echoed throughout the building as though some incumbent in the crypt had woken up and seen the cobwebs. And there it was again, this time louder than before.

'So?' answered the vicar to Arabella's inquisitive look. 'We have a ghost…..'

Arabella implored him to be silent then listened again, but the noise had stopped, the only sound in the church being the pitiful moaning and clicking of a tongue as the vicar tested each of his teeth for movement. She stood up and patted him kindly on the shoulder then walked across to the stone grill that served as a window to the outside.

'How far do you think it is from here to my house?' she asked, much to the vicar's surprise, whose capacity for small talk was limited by the sound of his mouth fizzing like a damp spoon of Epsom salts.

'What? Oh, I don't know; about a couple of hundred yards if that. You're back wall extends as far as my garden.'

'That's what I thought...hardly any distance at all.' She ran her fingers through the dust on the frame leaving behind a trace of hastily sketched algebra.

'I have another question,' she asked. 'It's about the damp in the crypt; has it always been so bad? It's like a swamp down there.'

'Do you actually expect an answer Miss Pike?' complained the vicar, 'because you certainly choose your moments to talk about the plumbing; and may I say, just for the record, that I take a poor view of people flaunting their explosives in public. I could have been blown to pieces with that damned marmalade of yours. Look at me, I can't stop shaking.'

Arabella dismissed his suffering with a shrug of her shoulders and walked back to the belfry steps, her calculations complete.

'I wouldn't advise staying up here for much longer; things are going to get very noisy, very soon. If you value your safety, then I suggest you go home at once. I intend to blow up your crypt.'

The vicar couldn't believe his ears. 'You Vandal!' he shouted, 'you Harpy! You Witch!'

Outside by the barricade, Professor Broadbent was either very brave or very stupid. It mattered very little in the long run. In the eyes of George Stubbins and Bill Hicken there could be only one possible outcome; a sprouting of swan's wings, the plucking of a harp and a general upward movement towards the heavens. The foolish man had challenged Stench to a duel and was now flexing his limbs and adopting the most exaggerated of fencing postures (courtesy of *The Masked Musketeer* at the Alhambra, Grubdale).

The first part of the professor's plan had come to nought. Vermyn Stench had refused to discard his cane in favour of a sword. Instead, he had held the weapon secure under his left arm and had pulled out a vicious, long blade from its centre; the damned device wasn't so much a wand as a Swiss Army knife. The professor's only chance now lay in a fight to the finish. He had instructed those of the Sisterhood fit enough to stand to blast his opponent with spells as soon as he had sliced through his arm. The chances of achieving this were slim, a probability driven home by the sight of Stench lazily skewering moths onto his blade as though he was preparing a kebab.

The two duellists walked out into the centre of the street under the only gas-light, their arms extended and the tips of their swords shaking ever so slowly. Their eyes were focussed on each other's expression, waiting for the tell-tale flick of an eyebrow or twitch of a lip that would herald a wild thrust or hack of the sword. Even the sound of an explosion from the church grounds caused them only to blink.

Stench was the first to attack. He tested the professor's defence by thrusting and swinging his blade repeatedly forward, forcing his opponent to parry the blows and shuffle backwards towards the barricade. But it was not to be an easy fight. There was skill or else blind panic in the professor's handling of the sword, and soon it was Stench's turn to defend his life as he fell back to the pub under a tirade of flashing steel.

A few of the soldier rats re-appeared outside the broken window of the pub and looked on, concerned as their leader fought his temporary retreat. This was unexpected, unnerving, for while soldier rats were renowned amongst their own for cruelty and cunning, any little tap on the shoulder would empty their bladders. They chattered nervously on the subject of losing, and then fell silent as Vermyn stumbled then found his feet again. It was too much excitement to take on a belly-full of warm ale. A little underhand assistance was required and as soon as possible if the 'day' was to be saved. One of the soldier rats raised his firearm and aimed the long barrel at Professor Broadbent's head. But the 'click' of the hammer being pulled back alerted his boss. Vermyn Stench span full circle in a blur of movement and the unfortunate soldier rat, separated neatly at the middle into two halves, fell to the floor in a spray of blood. It was to be a fair fight, at least on Stench's part; not out of any gentlemanly honour, but his right as leader of the pack to be the executioner.

Professor Broadbent nodded to Vermyn, acknowledging this noble if not surprising trait in his opponent's character. To be shot in the head, he thought, seemed preferable to having his stomach perforated by a dirty blade, for the professor was now panting, feeling his age and pessimistic of the outcome. He wiped his brow, and raised his sword again, adopting the stance of Sir Rodney Chumley in the final Act of *The Masked Musketeer*. It was the perfect position from which to slice a few candles or else spell out the odd letter or two on a linen shirt. Dammit but the creature was laughing at him, knocking the tip of his blade away with his own and egging him on to the attack. No, this was not the time to be a pessimist. Stench was merely an animal, a creature of instinct, whilst *he*, a professor and published at that, was a man of logic, inspiration *and*, as he stamped down hard on the ratman's foot and followed through with a glass-shattering knee to the groin, sufficiently academic to realise his own limitations. He took advantage of his opponent's sudden need to cross his legs and suck in air like a whale, to slice his sword around and down in a vicious arc. But instead of separating Stench from his protective talisman, the blade missed the claw and hit the ground at the creature's feet, shattering on impact. There was a terrible pause as both combatants stared at each other, their noses touching, and then with a speed that belied his age, Professor Broadbent jumped backwards and ran as fast as he could in the direction of the barricade. Talisman or not, the professor had only one choice, to blow the rat-thing to smithereens and to hell with the village.

There was a second explosion, louder than the first, and the ground beneath the professor's feet shook with such violence that he stumbled to the floor. A few of the Sisterhood scrambled on top of the barricade and shouted at the professor to get up and hurry. Vermyn Stench had come to his senses and was making ready his attack, limping forward with his pack of soldier rats and shouting and kicking them from behind. Professor Broadbent scrambled to his feet and sprinted the few remaining yards to safety, aware of knives being thrown past his head and claws grabbing at the back of his coat. George and Bill Hicken took aim with two of the remaining shotguns and managed to bring down the front-runners, but the rest of the mob leapt over their fallen comrades and flung themselves at the barricade.

It was a desperate fight for the defenders to hold their position. Any thought of success was chastened by the wasted opportunity of the second explosion. Wherever its centre was, it had been too early and too ineffectual. One party, led by those of the Sisterhood who could still stand firm on top of the barricade, was attempting to beat down the soldier rats, while the others, led by the professor, George and Bill Hicken, threw stones at Stench whenever he opened his mouth to cast a spell. It was a difficult strategy to maintain for they were trying to save their strength for one last charge, a suicidal attack to wrestle the protective talisman from his grasp. There was a shout from some of the Sisters to make ready as part of the barricade collapsed under the onslaught.

'Well, gentlemen,' said the professor, 'Let us not die strangers. Arbutus Broadbent at your service.'

'It's a pleasure to have met you. Bill Hicken's the name, Sergeant Bill Hicken of the 1st Grubdale Rifles.'

'A proud and worthy regiment Bill, and you would be?' inquired the professor holding his hand out to George.

'George Stubbins, landlord of that wonderful establishment opposite. If there's anything left of the place tonight then I would be honoured to stand you a pint or two, and maybe a whiskey.'

The emotion of the moment was getting the better of the three gentlemen. They stood in a circle, shaking hands and patting each other on the back until one of the Sisterhood pointed out that the entire barricade had collapsed and now would be as good a time as any for some decisive action.

'All for one...'

'....and one for all!' the three cried as they lowered their shoulders and charged forward. But instead of colliding into the pack of attacking rats and knocking Vermyn Stench to the floor, they found themselves stumbling down an ever steepening slope, deeper and deeper underground.

The soldier rats skidded to a halt before a large hole that had suddenly appeared in front, a hole that was growing larger by the minute as the surface of the street crumbled and poured away from sight. On the other side rested the remaining band of Sisters, some standing and panting for breath, while the more bruised and battered looked on in disbelief. It was too dark to see to the bottom of the hole, but something was worrying the rats. They refused to creep around and continue their attack but stood firm, hurling insults and shaking their knives and swords at the enemy. Stench pushed his way through from the back and with his sword now safely ensconced within his cane, twisted the silver claw on top. A bright green flame appeared, and now crouching on all fours, Stench swung the torch this way and that, trying to make out any movement below. But it was more than moths that were attracted to the flame. There was a sudden animal roar as Arabella shot out from the hole and hung suspended in the air above the crowd. From behind her appeared the professor and his two companions, their legs held curiously apart as though they were balanced on some invisible horse. George was in the middle although facing in the wrong direction, his forehead banging against that of Bill Hicken's as whatever they were sitting on rose high then fell low with an alarming regularity.

Arabella leant forward and clasped her arms around some invisible neck as a jet of flame discharged and hit the ground. Two soldier rats caught fire and ran amok in all directions, but were merely pushed away or hacked at with swords in a general panic to escape. Some of their colleagues were being cast high up in the night sky, and instead of falling back to the ground with a bump were being churned and rolled about in an increasingly horrid fashion.

Down on the ground the Sisterhood were in fits of delight. They held on to each other and jumped up and down screaming with joy. They waved to Miss Pike and pointed to the faint outline of something large hovering overhead. The *Big Secret* was a secret no more. Arabella had discovered a Great Wyrm, one of the stately Wyrms of England. It was just as she had told them in their meeting in Grubdale, and now everything was possible.

'Well done Miss Pike,' called out an emotional Professor Broadbent, edging himself carefully along the beast's long neck till he was sitting behind Arabella, 'I thought for a moment we were all finished, but ten out of ten for my marmalade I think.'

'And my research,' added Arabella rather annoyed with the professor's brusque dismissal, 'not to mention intuition, fortitude and a great sense of timing.'

'Yes, yes, it goes without saying Miss Pike' he interrupted, taking the chance to examine the outline of the beast and pat it lovingly on the side. 'My, my but this is an impressive specimen. Just one minor complaint; can't you get the Wyrm to stop chewing up these soldier rats; its Vermyn Stench we need to concentrate on, and I can't see where he's got to from here.'

'I don't think it's as easy as that,' said Arabella. 'It's not as though I'm in control. I only hope there are enough large rats to satisfy the Wyrm's hunger. I suggest we leave well alone for the moment unless *we* are next on the menu.'

'Well, you know best but it seems a pity to get this far only to let Stench escape, especially since our friend's fire's stoked up.' He smiled as another jet of flame caused panic amongst the rats below. 'I can't imagine Stench having *any* protection from that.'

The professor may have been correct. Stench had taken advantage of the confusion and slaughter to retreat into hiding in the shadows. His mission was a failure, and all that remained was for him to return home in disgrace. But to do so empty-handed? That way led to pain and retribution. No, there was the slightest chance that he could save face with Tarantulas Spleen and maybe regain the initiative. He kept to the dark corners and back yards of the village avoiding the bloodshed and commotion on the high street, then re-emerged some distance from the barricade. In front of him walked a solitary member of the Sisterhood, limping and making her way past the church, unaware that Vermyn Stench was close behind. This was the chance he needed. He got down on all fours and arched his back. His skin split apart, and a pair of leathery wings unfurled and flapped tentatively in the night breeze, and then he pounced. He charged towards the unsuspecting woman and grabbing her around the waist, soared upwards into the sky. The Sister cursed as she felt herself being dragged aloft. She pummelled the arm squeezing her around the waist and kicked back with the heels of her boots, but Stench had too tight a hold. He covered her mouth with his claw and immediately wished he hadn't. The finest pair of dentures this side of the Pennines bit down deep and worried his flesh like a shark. Stench roared out in pain, and immediately the ears of the Great Wyrm pricked up, and its head swung around. The Wyrm spat out a large fireball that collided with the steeple and exploded into a starburst of light covering Vermyn with a shower of sparks and burning gas.

'There he is!' shouted Arabella pointing towards the enemy, and the professor looked over her shoulder to see the winged figure of Stench some way off in the distance. He appeared a desperate creature trying to shake off the biting grip of the dentures and put out a number of fires that were spitting and smouldering in his fur. There was a bounce and a stream of unintelligible abuse as a toothless woman rolled to a stop by the vicarage.

'Is there a way we can make this Wyrm fly any faster?' complained the professor as Arabella urged the transparent beast forward in pursuit. 'We don't seem to be making headway.'

'It's probably stiff as well as hungry. I shouldn't worry. We'll soon catch up with our prey.'

The professor kept his immediate thoughts to himself. He was unconvinced. He had not expected this sudden change in events and now the flying Stench was disappearing quickly out of sight. 'Then let us press on regardless,' he said. 'At least we know where he's headed.'

Chapter Seven

THE GROUSE SHOOT

Bethesda Chubb was cold, wet and miserable and her companion on the moor, Miss Trout, felt no better. Their tweed outfits were damp, they stank of soot and to make matters worse Miss Trout had a bag of boiled sweets she was keeping to herself. The two ladies sat in silence huddled around a smoking fire, each sporting a black eye and a cut lip. They had argued over the machine gun, what to shoot at, when and who should pull the trigger, and after a sharp exchange of blows had put these questions on hold until tempers cooled down. They blew on their hands and stamped their feet as the fire sputtered to nothing, oblivious of a khaki-clad figure striding purposely through the heather.

It was one of those unfortunate coincidences, a strange happenstance that alters the telling of a tale. Captain Hilary Dashing was enjoying the crisp morning air, and where better than on Grimspittle Moor. Here was a happy man with the promise of a weekend's sport ahead, and even if he was a guest of the peculiar Mr Crispian Day, ex-Member of Parliament and well-known odd-bod, what was a little village gossip to the chance of bagging a brace or two of grouse. True, his host was 'not himself'. An unfortunate illness of a feminine kind had struck him down mid-career or according to Bethesda's watch, about five minutes into his inaugural speech on the stupidity of allowing women the vote. But one had to be charitable. These were modern times and the gentleman's hospitality was renowned. Such a pity about the other guests, two businessmen from Berlin given to whispering behind their newspapers and hogging all the port. He was damned if he would let them bag the best of the birds. So he had set his alarm clock for six in the morning, had breakfasted light and after rousing his beloved black Labrador from in front of the kitchen fire, had crept quietly out of the lodge to be the first on the moor.

The captain looked at his watch and waited for his bagman to catch up, an exhausted Private Oldfield dragging a sack of shotguns behind him. 'There, I thought you were out of condition,' he said. 'Three miles and you're gasping like an old man. A disgraceful state you've let yourself get into. As soon as this weekend's over it's the gym for you.'

It was all the poor soldier could do to nod in agreement. He dropped the sack and lay back in the heather, too tired to fend off the wet nose and tongue of the inquisitive Labrador. The captain looked on impatiently. 'I trust you slept well?' he asked.

'To be honest Sir, no,' answered Private Oldfield. 'I was woken up in the middle of the night by giggling and the smell of cheap scent. It reminded me of that horrible woman.'

'Oh, I shouldn't worry about that,' dismissed the captain, embarrassed. 'It was most probably our host, a harmless gentleman but a puzzling condition. It doesn't do to talk about these things you understand, not since he lost his seat in the House.'

Private Oldfield understood perfectly, the first thing he had noticed on arriving at the lodge was Mr Day's cleavage and his peculiar choice of clothes. It appeared that kilts were being worn long this season with sporrans on a strap around the shoulder.

'Mind you,' continued the captain. 'If he does sneak into your bedroom then talk about rugger. He's perfectly safe on sport; just don't let him change the conversation to Shakespeare. One moment he's the Prince of Denmark, the next the clothes are off and he's floating like Ophelia in the bathtub, shocking behaviour but a generous spirit. I find a pistol under the pillow helps.'

Private Oldfield shuddered and made a note to lock the bedroom door.

'Get to your feet then, we've the whole day ahead and no sign of those boorish Germans.'

Captain Dashing searched through the sack for a suitable weapon. 'What about this?' he suggested, pulling up the barrel of some monstrous rifle. Private Oldfield shook his head; there were no elephants in Derbyshire. 'Damn, well maybe this one, just the ticket for the morning's sport, don't you think?' He exchanged the larger rifle with one more appropriate; a single-barrelled fowling piece that could bring down an albatross yet leave something left over for the sandwiches. Private Oldfield nodded in agreement.

'Excellent, now if you wouldn't mind, take this stick, walk over there and thrash it about in the heather like so.' The captain swung a bamboo cane a few times at his feet and stepped back in surprise as a hare stood up and ran for cover. He stared at his Labrador in disappointment. 'Blimey old girl, you missed that one. Look lively there.'

Private Oldfield took the cane and walked some distance away, but not too far. From the size of the captain's gun, he stood a better chance of survival if he could be seen as well as the quarry. A brace of grouse broke cover, their wings slapping noisily against the still morning air until with a single shot one fell to earth and bounced in front of the hide. Before the Labrador had chance to waddle over and investigate, the body of the lifeless bird was sliced to pieces by a tirade of machinegun fire. The captain looked on in amazement then removed the spent cartridge from the chamber of his gun and read the label. *Pluggham and Splatter, Powders of Distinction.'* Well, he thought, one can hardly argue with that, explosive shot and on a slow fuse too. Whatever will they think of next? He reloaded the shotgun and gave the signal for Private Oldfield to continue. It didn't take long before a second brace of birds took to the air. The captain swung his gun to his shoulder and let fire, but this time Miss Trout had had enough. She was fed up with the bossy Miss Chubb and was determined to spoil her fun. She threw the small pot of explosive in the direction of the falling grouse, folded her arms and smiled innocently at her companion. Bethesda pulled the trigger. There was a tremendous thunderclap, a rush of air and what seemed like half the peat bogs of Ireland descending in shreds from the sky. Captain Dashing removed his cartridge belt and placed it very, very carefully on the ground. Powders of distinction or not, *Pluggham and Splatter* was too strong a brew for his taste. He caught hold of the shivering Labrador's collar and tiptoed backwards.

'Sir!' Private Oldfield shouted, stunned and covered in peat but still managing to stumble forward to the captain. 'Head for cover, it's an ambush!'

'What on earth?' exclaimed Captain Dashing, and then noticed the outline of Bethesda and Miss Trout dragging themselves out of the ruined hide and carrying the machine gun between them.

'Good God, Oldfield, I see what you mean. You attract those blasted women like flies.'

Before Private Oldfield could answer, there was a scream as one of the ladies was knocked to the ground by what seemed like a gigantic bat swooping down from the sky. Captain Dashing and Private Oldfield looked on as the large creature retreated its wings then set about Miss Trout with its cane.

'Do you think that 'thing' is one of ours, Oldfield? Those blighters at the Ministry are secretive about their gadgets.'

'I don't know Sir, but whose ever it is, it doesn't like spies.'

The 'thing' was Stench, swiping and chasing Miss Trout. He gave up the pursuit and returned to the unconscious Bethesda Chubb.

'Oh dear, Oldfield, perhaps we should avert our eyes, prizes of war and all that.'

To their shame, the two continued to stare as Stench lifted Miss

Chubb over his shoulder and walked away. Then the most peculiar of things happened, the creature just disappeared. Captain Dashing rubbed his eyes and searched the moor again but there was nothing to see, no mist, no hole to fall into and no creature. The hairs on the back of the Labrador stood up as she began to growl and pull away from her master.

'I know, old girl, bloody peculiar. What do you make of that Oldfield?'

Private Oldfield shook his head and shrugged his shoulders, there could be no explanation. Whatever had happened, the figure had simply vanished. But there was no time to debate the point. The Sisterhood were beginning to arrive. 'Quick Sir,' he whispered, grabbing hold of the captain's arm, 'not a sound, we must hide behind this wall.'

'What did you say? Is that you pulling at my arm? Unhand me at once!' Private Oldfield managed to throw the captain to the ground as a number of shadows passed overhead. 'I'm sorry Sir, but if they see us here, we're in trouble.'

'Quite right,' mumbled Captain Dashing, his mouth pressed against the damp soil, 'but get off my back, will you. I can hardly breathe.'

Private Oldfield obeyed and drew the Labrador to him, soothing it with quiet words so that it wouldn't bark. The captain raised his head then turned to one side to get a better look. 'Well I never,' he said in surprise. 'They've brought their entire family. Quick thinking Private, well done.'

The advance party of the Sisterhood, fresh from fighting and bruised and battered as a result, floated down from the sky and landed by a large, deep crater. It was all that remained of the small pot of explosive thrown by Miss Trout. They walked around the crater's edge, searching for their companions, but all they could find was the machine gun with its barrel still hot. They feared for the worst and lowered their heads in silence. A figure stood up and stumbled towards them. It was Miss Trout, dazed but overjoyed to see her friends, and from what the captain and Private Oldfield could see from her wild hand movements, was attempting to explain what had happened.

'Are you telling me that these women were in the hotel?' the captain whispered.

'Yes, Sir.'

'Well, they look foreign. No self-respecting English woman would have muscles like that. We must inform the Ministry at once, these blighters can fly.' He said this with no surprise, just a matter-of-fact reporting of the 'obvious'. 'But why should they try and kill us, that's the mystery?' The captain, never the brightest spark at college, returned his attention to Miss Trout. 'Do you think she's told them about us? I can't tell from this distance. At least she's not pointing over here.'

'I don't know, Sir. If she has, then we'll know soon enough.'

'Quite, well I have a pistol, what about you?'

'I'd better crawl back and get the sack.'

'Good idea…'

The Labrador began to whimper and buried its muzzle deep in Private Oldfield's armpit.

'What's the matter old girl, has something scared you?'

Something had, an oppressive swirling and snorting of the air that was growing ever louder. The captain heard the noise and turned his head to look up at the morning sky. He swore out of amazement then nudged Private Oldfield in the ribs. 'Forget the guns,' he said. 'I think we're in more trouble than we thought.' The two soldiers lay speechless as the giant Wyrm hovered overhead.

It is amazing the effect a light breakfast can have, particularly if you've slept for thousands of years with only shreds of meat stuck between your teeth. 'Playful,' would be a reasonable word to explain the Wyrm's behaviour, but only if you were an experienced jockey. Arabella and the professor were not, and as for poor Bill Hicken and George Stubbins, they were last seen helping each other out of the River Wryggle some miles back. It had everything to do with looping-the-loop and a sudden urge to skim the surface of a river while flying upside down to gargle.

'Do you think we could land now?' the professor asked. He was covering his mouth with a silk-spotted handkerchief and looking a little green. 'I feel the need to step on firm ground.'

Arabella looked over her shoulder and nodded, a similar handkerchief pressed against her pale face. The Wyrm was not the easiest of creatures to steer let alone keep in a straight line and was now flying around in a circle obviously interested in the large crater still smoking below.

'I really would appreciate an end to this flight, Miss Pike, as quickly as possible please.'

Arabella turned to face the front, but there was little she could do to take control. She'd tried all the obvious commands like 'right', 'left' and 'not in the chimney pots', but the beast had ignored her and taken a circuitous route around the local scenery before arriving on the moor. Now, with both of its passengers feeling the worse for their journey, the Wyrm grew suddenly bored and descended with alarming speed to land with a bump in the middle of the crater.

'Not a form of transport I care to try again,' Professor Broadbent said, his face squashed up against the back of Arabella's hair. 'But well done all the same.' He attempted to climb off the Wyrm's neck, but on releasing his grip found himself sliding backwards at alarming speed until he hit the ground with a thump.

'Are you hurt?' inquired Arabella. It took a few moments before the professor could talk, but from the look of his face and the way he walked around the base of the crater, he probably was. The Wyrm lowered its head so that Arabella slid forward onto its nose, then with a gentle flick the creature cast her up in the air. She performed the perfect somersault and floated safely down.

The professor was unimpressed. 'Don't stand there gawping like a group of fishwives', he moaned, still feeling the pain from sliding down a banister of never-ending bookends. 'Will someone help me out of this hole?' He was ignored. The ladies were praising Arabella, pointing at the great Wyrm and crying and laughing for joy. 'Thank you, most kind!' he muttered and tried to climb the steep slope. Yet each time he neared the top he would hear someone giggle and if by magic the soil would crumble away and he would slide back down to the bottom.

One of the sisters took pity and pulled the professor up by the back of his jacket. He grumbled and snorted, but it was only a half-hearted annoyance, for here before him stood one of the stately Wyrms of England. 'Ladies, where are our manners,' the professor said pushing through the crowd. 'We are in the presence of Royalty.'

A change had come across the Wyrm; it had digested its breakfast. 'So what?' you might say, particularly if you were a young father sponging the shoulder of your cardigan, 'where's the surprise in that?' But the professor knew different, for while babies ooze at the edges when full to their cheeks, Wyrms turn opaque, particularly after their first meal of the millennium. After an explosive burp and a rumbling of the stomach, the Wyrm was visible to all.

'Your Majesty,' the professor said in greeting, bending low, 'You are indeed a Queen amongst Wyrms.' The Wyrm blinked, sniffed the jacket of this obsequious gentleman then accepted his flattery with a slight nod of her head. She was magnificent, for all the years she had slept in the earth her scales shone blue and silver, and the circle of horns on her head glowed as a luminous crown. Miss Trout pushed her way to the front, tears streaming down her cheek.

'Oh Professor, is it true, can it be a royal Wyrm after all? I do wish Bethesda was here to see it.'

The professor scanned the crowd of ladies then took Miss Trout to one side. 'And why isn't she here?' he asked. 'Not off on one of her little crusades again? Don't tell me, she's at the hunting lodge making trouble for us all. You realise who owns the property, the unfortunate Mr Day. I do hope she leaves him alone; the first curse was bad enough…'

'Oh no, Professor, you've got it wrong. You're being most unfair. Poor Bethesda didn't go anywhere near the place. She's been kidnapped by the enemy.' Miss Trout dabbed at her eyes with an old sock and explained what had happened.

'Stench has taken her prisoner?' he snapped. 'Is that what you're trying to say?'

Miss Trout nodded. 'I tried my best, but…'

'And what of the machine gun and explosive, I see you've made good use of them. Did you miss?'

Miss Trout silenced the professor with a single look. It was as if all his life's misdemeanours had been pulled out of his trouser pockets and placed on display on the teacher's desk. 'I'm…I'm sure you fought bravely,' he stammered. 'How could I have thought otherwise? This is terrible news, the poor girl, what will they do to her?'

Miss Trout waited for the full effect of her stare before shrugging her shoulders and burying her face in her hands. 'I dare not think,' she sobbed.

'Neither dare I, but we must face facts. This puts the whole of our plan into jeopardy. To be honest Miss Trout, I'm at a loss as to what to do next.' The professor turned around to hide his anger and was startled to find Arabella standing in front.

'The choice is obvious,' she whispered. 'We must close the wyrmhole and forget about her.'

'But that would be heartless.'

'We have to be practical. Our mission won't be a secret once Spleen gets his claws into Miss Chubb. She's bound to talk, and it's as you said, we must protect our backs. There will be other portals to guide us home, secret paths the sorcerer knows nothing of. Let us close this one and hope for the best. A single Wyrm is hardly a rebellion. We will need others to rally the people to our cause. Until then let us continue with the search.'

It was the professor's turn to shrug his shoulders. 'You're most probably right, Miss Pike. But we are still abandoning one of our own. Perhaps you could explain it to the others. I haven't the stomach for it.' He sat down on the edge of the crater and let his tears fall, overwhelmed with a sadness.

'Isn't she the most marvellous of creatures in the world,' sighed Miss Trout, sitting down next to the professor. If she meant the Wyrm, then he agreed. He nodded his head not being able to speak for the lump in his throat. 'It's strange isn't it,' she continued, 'that something as beautiful as this should choose to hide away for all eternity, and why here, such a cold and wet place to fall asleep.

'She would have understood, you know.'

'Who would have?' the professor asked.

'Bethesda, silly.'

'Why are you talking about her as though she was dead?' snorted Arabella. 'She's a tough old boot. Who knows what may happen when she wakes up. One thing's for certain, she wouldn't want us like this, crying and sobbing and wasting precious time. Come on, we've too much to do.

Convincing the Wyrm to climb out of that hole and close the portal would be a useful start, wouldn't you say Professor? We don't want to stay here and attract attention.'

It seemed an odd thing to say, to attract attention, odder still if Arabella had known about the soldiers.

'This is incredible,' whispered Captain Dashing. 'Everyone seems to be flying save for us. And that machine, it's gigantic. It can't be one of ours, not with those damned women at the helm.'

'It could be, Sir. We can't be certain. As you said yourself, the Ministry doesn't tell you everything. What if the machine is ours and it's being stolen before our eyes? Surely we should do something?'

'I'd like to know what – there's only two of us and a bloody tea dance of them. No Private Oldfield, there's little sense in getting killed. We shall stay put and see what happens, and then we shall file a report. You haven't a pen on hand have you, or a piece of paper?' Again, an unfortunate coincidence, for these were the exact same words being spoken in German from behind another wall.

The peculiar Mr Crispian Day was feeling even more peculiar. It seemed the 'curse' had lifted. He awoke late in the morning to find on sitting up in bed, two fluffy slippers, a floral dressing gown and, horror upon horror, a very large teddy bear in a tutu staring at him from across the room. He shook his head, bewildered, but the awful objects remained where they were, screaming at him with their femininity. He tried to remember the exact details of the previous evening, even the past month, but his memory was a coddled blur. It was as if he was Rip Van Winkle waking up from a hundred-year sleep, and with a six-foot beard and toenails like lollipop sticks. He rolled out of bed and, kicking the offending slippers across the room, walked to the adjoining bathroom shouting for Moffat, his valet, to hurry up with the rose petal tea and grapefruit. He stopped suddenly outside the door. Rose petal tea and grapefruit, what on earth was he thinking of? He shook the sleep from his brain and was just about to kick the bathroom door open when the dreadful possibility that the room may be occupied came to him. He knocked tentatively, twice, and then hearing no answer pushed the door gently open and looked around.

Surely this was not his room? There were enough bottles of perfume to sweeten the Nile. He tiptoed in then jumped back in surprise at his reflection in the mirror. Some scoundrel had dressed him up in the most flimsy of silk pyjamas, and as for his hair? He couldn't for the life of him think why it hadn't been cut. A disgrace it was, almost to his shoulders. He ripped away the pyjamas, but nothing could have prepared him for the underwear beneath.

Moffat heard a scream coming from his Master's bathroom as he climbed the stairs with the breakfast tray. Here we go again, he thought. Any more peculiar behaviour from Mr Day and he would hand in his notice.

'Moffat,' shouted the confused Crispian standing at the top of the flight of stairs. 'Can we account for these?' He was holding out a pair of Parisian undergarments torn down the middle in the panic to get them off. Moffat stood for a while, his eyes filling up with tears.

'Oh Sir, it does me good to see you like this. Back to your old self you are and that's a fact. These past months have been a nightmare. Leave those rags at the top of the stairs and I'll look out your woollen combinations, just like the good old days.'

'Moffat, I haven't a clue what you're on about. Explain yourself man.'

'Your figure Sir, it seems to have regained its shape; and your voice, quite back to its sonorous tone.'

Crispian looked down at his chest and tried to push to the back of his mind a particularly horrid memory that had suddenly sprung forth.

'If I may say so Sir, these past few months have been as if some witch had put a spell on you, and such a terrible spell. Your symptoms had the doctors flummoxed.' Moffat walked past his employer and placed the breakfast tray down on the dressing table. 'Just say the word Sir and I'll clear away these baubles.'

Crispian followed him back into the bedroom. 'What baubles?' he asked.

'It's a pleasure to hear those words. Why, but these baubles of course.' Moffat picked up handfuls of pearl necklaces draped across the furniture along with a scattering of silk scarves and feather boas.

'They're mine?'

'Unfortunately, yes.'

Another memory, more flamboyant than the first, bubbled to the surface. Crispian covered his face with his hands and groaned aloud. 'Please Moffat, take them away at once!' he hissed.

'Certainly Sir and what about the…' Moffat hesitated to say the name. '…teddy bear? Should I remove that as well?'

Crispian could only nod in reply as he sank slowly to the carpet. The curse may have been lifted but the memories were returning, each as potent as a punch in the stomach.

'Very good Sir.' Moffat tiptoed out of the room and threw the teddy bear down the stairs with obvious glee. What a wonderful morning this was turning out. All he need do was rid his employer of the dresses in the wardrobe and his day would be complete.

'Moffat,' Crispian cried out in a pathetic voice. 'Remind me, do we have any guests?'

'Four Sir, two young soldiers and two German businessmen, should I tell them to go?'

'I think that would best. I seem to have written something very unfortunate in my diary.'

To close a wyrmhole in space seems hardly the most difficult of tasks, one merely asks whoever opened the door to shut it as there's a draught. But try telling that to a physicist with an eye on the best seller list, or a certain Captain Dashing hiding behind a wall on Grimspittle Moor.

'Oldfield, are my eyes deceiving me or does that flying contraption look like a dragon?'

'I rather think it does, Sir.'

'Hah, then foreign it is! You wouldn't catch one of our boffins disguising something as a creature that never existed. Bound to cause notice, that would.'

'Perhaps it's what they intend, Sir, to cause terror and panic.'

'Nonsense Oldfield, all that paint and chiselling fools nobody. You'll be telling me it breathes fire next...'

Hardly had the captain finished speaking than the Wyrm reared up on its hind legs and shot forth a continuous jet of flame.

'Well done Your Majesty,' encouraged Professor Broadbent pointing towards the portal. 'Just a few seconds more and we'll have it sealed shut.'

Private Oldfield was shocked. He had never heard his captain swear or have him fling his arms around his neck and cry out for mother. 'Steady on Sir,' he whispered pushing the captain away. But the man was in a panic. Captain Dashing had jumped to his feet and was sprinting back to the lodge as though the bats of hell were chasing him, and not a fat black Labrador making heavy weather of the exercise. 'It's only a machine,' muttered Private Oldfield. He stood up from the ground, then thinking better of it set off after the captain at breakneck speed, hardly noticing the two terrified Germans fleeing from the moor in the opposite direction.

'Well, that's that then,' said Professor Broadbent. 'No chance of anything getting through from the other side now.' He was standing in front of what was once a wyrmhole but was now just a warm patch of air in a grey morning sky. The Wyrm was munching on a gorse bush to take the taste of fire from its mouth, whilst the remainder of the Sisterhood were tending to each other's wounds or else taking the opportunity for a quick nap.

'Care for a cigar?' Arabella asked, lighting up one of her infamous cheroots with a click of her fingers. 'It will help you stay awake.'

'I thought they had the opposite effect? No thank you Miss Pike, I'll stick to my sweets.' The professor rummaged in his jacket pocket and brought out a paper bag full of humbugs. He popped one in his mouth and rattled it around on his teeth. 'She's rather large, isn't she?' he said.

Arabella blew out a long trail of purple smoke and smiled. 'I thought Wyrms were.'

'I know, I know. It's just that one forgets, not the size perhaps, but the shape. Things are never the same in books. Still,' he said holding out his hands and making a frame with them to look through. 'There is a certain resemblance, I suppose.'

'She looks exactly the same as in the book. What are you mumbling on about? A Wyrm is a Wyrm is a Wyrm.'

'Aha! Not exactly Miss Pike, and therein lies the solution. I just hope we can find enough paint. Two coats should do the job.' The professor popped another humbug in his mouth and hummed merrily to himself as he sucked on his sweet.

Arabella puffed away on her cigar. 'I haven't a clue what you mean,' she said then lay back in the heather to rest. No doubt the professor would explain in due course. 'Due course' proved shortly after, when Arabella had fallen fast asleep, and Professor Broadbent had come to the end of his humbug.

'You do realise Miss Pike that Her Majesty can't stay here on the moor. Someone might see her and then where would we be? No, there will be enough trouble when last night's adventure gets into the papers. It's best for everyone if we keep her on the move.'

Arabella opened one eye and looked at the Wyrm. 'You may find that difficult,' she said. 'It would seem Her Majesty is making herself at home.'

The crater was proving just the ticket for a sleepy Wyrm. The creature turned around a few times in the deep hollow then, with an almost human look of contentment, lay down in the soft peat and tucked its head under its wing.

'Oh dear no,' cried the professor. 'This won't do at all. If she falls asleep now, she may stay like that for years. WAKE UP YOUR MAJESTY,' he shouted. 'RISE AND SHINE!'

The Wyrm thought little of this. It raised its snout above the edge of the crater and blew a snort of protest at the bumptious professor covering the esteemed Arbutus Broadbent in a thick coat of soot. 'Well, well,' he said, trying to maintain an air of dignity. 'At least there's no possibility of me being recognised. And wasn't it lucky I put on my best suit.'

Arabella found it difficult not to laugh. 'Come on,' she said. 'There's no harm done. Think of it as a disguise. You can walk behind and be my shadow.'

'Very funny Miss Pike, but as always you have hit the nail on the head. That is what the paint will be for, a disguise.

'Ladies, you see before you not a great Wyrm but a humble giraffe, not worthy of comment.'

'A giraffe, in Derbyshire? It amounts to the same thing, surely. People will notice.'

'Again you are mistaken. The idea is not as silly as you may think. Haven't you heard of the famous Grubdale Park Zoo?'

'No,'

'Then you are in for a rare treat, and Her Majesty here, a more varied diet.' The professor hugged himself and smiled at the pure genius of his plan. 'You know Miss Pike. I think I will have one of those cigars after all.'

Continue the adventure in
EDUCATING CREATURES
Part Two of THE TROUBLE WITH WYRMS Trilogy
by
Mike Williams

LIST OF CHARACTERS

The Sisterhood – a once important guild of witches from the planet Vivarium, protectors of the exiled Prince of Wyrm and now seekers of the great Wyrms of antiquity.

Arabella Pike – senior member of the Sisterhood and life-long companion of Rowena Carp with, as Arabella would be the first to admit, the mental scars to show for it. Perhaps the most serious member of the guild but that's not saying much. Lives in the village of Sodden-on-the-Bog and as our story begins has been excavating the cellars of her house to discover the source of a deep rumbling, snoring noise that keeps her awake at night. She has been known to keep a cave squid or two in her cellar to deter burglars.

Rowena Carp – a flamboyant member of the Sisterhood given to pouncing on Scottish pipers and declaring her love. Lifelong companion of Arabella Pike with, as Rowena would be the first to admit, the mental scars to show for it. She is the only member of the Sisterhood to keep a familiar, which in her case is a Jellico she discovered in a very cheap restaurant, lying on her salad and with an apple in its mouth. In remembrance of a past affair and of a similar posture, she has named the Jellico Demetrios.

Bethesda Chubb – the youngest member of the Sisterhood and the most erratic, given to fighting at the least opportunity and declaring her admiration for Emmeline Pankhurst and the Suffragettes. She is often found wearing a necklace of dentures – prizes from numerous encounters with the London constabulary – and a policeman's helmet. She is fond of any weapon that makes a loud noise and shreds her enemies to jam and biscuits.

Demetrios – a Jellico from the forests of Tweeb and beloved companion of Rowena Carp. Resembles a fat pink poodle but breathes fire and would bite the hand off your arm if you offered him a dog biscuit.

Professor Arbutus Broadbent – the only male member of the Sisterhood on account of his very great intelligence and sobriety. Considers himself to be a man of science but is not averse to the odd spell or two as long as he is looking the other way.

Miss Wallace – Professor Broadbent's housekeeper of dubious history. She is rather fond of the Professor's sherry if only she could get her hands on the key to the tantalus.

George Stubbins – landlord of the only pub in the village of Sodden-on-the-Bog, 'The Lamb and Liver Fluke'; a very nosey individual who likes nothing better than to listen to village gossip and jump to the wrong conclusion about everything. He has a dog of limited intelligence, Scutt the terrier which he mistakenly believes to be the best ratter in the county.

Mrs Stubbins – George's long-suffering wife. She is often found packing her suitcase and 'going to her mother.'

William Hicken – one of George's oldest and faithful customers. He keeps a ferret called Old Sherlock down his trousers which he brings out to show at the least provocation. He is what is known in the village as a 'rustic character.'

Reverend Ainsley Cross – Vicar of the Parish of Sodden and keen amateur photographer. He likes nothing better than to drape his house cleaner in robes and flowers and make her 'smile at the birdie.'

Captain Hilary Dashing – Captain of the 1st Grubdale Rifles and erstwhile not-so-secret agent for the War Office.

Private William Oldfield – Private of the 1st Grubdale Rifles and erstwhile ever-so-not-so-secret agent for the War Office.

The Right Honourable Crispian Day – member of parliament for the area who on insulting the Suffragette movement in his inaugural speech to the house found himself in early retirement due to sudden and alarming changes to his appearance – mainly due to an unfortunate curse placed on him by Bethesda Chubb after reading his speech in the Daily Telegraph.

Moffat – Crispian Day's long-suffering valet.

Tarantulus Spleen – Terrible Sorcerer and ruler of Vivarium, usurper of the Throne of Wyrm, murderer, card sharp and downright nasty person altogether.

Vermyn Stench – Head of Spleen's Secret Service - half man, half rat, all bad.

The Blue Wyrm – one of the Stately Wyrms of England, an ancient race of dragons that have shaped the universe as we know it today, mostly by drilling wyrmholes in space and letting any old riff-raff through.

ABOUT THE AUTHOR

Mike Williams (1959 to one day when he's not looking) was born in the town of Market Harborough and due to a mix up with a local fortune teller was photographed for much of his first year in a dress. After moving to the Derbyshire Dales to escape the shame, he took to farming like a duck to liver pate and for many years seemed perpetually doused in manure, mostly from slipping on the cobbles or walking too near the cows at milking time. Educated at Buxton College, Chesterfield Art College and Trent Polytechnic, he threw away the wellington boots for a briefcase, was awarded a doctorate in 1986 and since then has lectured and published widely in plant physiology. He can be found waxing lyrical to students on the intimate contents of a leaf at Trinity College, Dublin or picking terrible fantasy football teams in his local pub 'The Villager' in Chapelizod. He is single with a cat, and a big one at that.

For more information on other books by Mike Williams then visit
www.facebook.com/Grubdale

Printed in Great Britain
by Amazon.co.uk, Ltd.,
Marston Gate.